RETURN OF THE DRAGONS

Gateskin Chronicles, Book 4

JANICE SPINA

PUBLISHED BY JANICE SPINA

COPYRIGHT 2025
JANICE SPINA
Londonderry, New Hampshire

COVER BY JOHN SPINA

ISBN (paperback) 979-8-9874646-5-6

Library of Congress Control Number: 2025913372

ACKNOWLEDGEMENTS

A very special thank you to my wonderful beta readers, Patricia Bradley, Michelle Clement James, Michele Rolfe and John Spina for working tirelessly to read and review my work and for their helpful input. Their assistance is invaluable and appreciated.

Thank you to my husband, John, for the beautiful cover and for all the dinners he cooked that made it possible for me to write.

DEDICATION

This book is dedicated to the memory of my best friend, Frances Stewart, who lost her life on June 16, 2025 from ovarian cancer. I miss her every day! May she rest in peace.

Table of Contents

RETURN OF THE DRAGONS 1

   Gateskin Chronicles, Book 4....................................1

PUBLISHED BY JANICE SPINA..............................2

ACKNOWLEDGEMENTS...................................4

DEDICATION..5

MAP OF NOELLA PROVINCE 10

CHARACTERS...11

CHAPTER ONE 23

CHAPTER TWO.......................................29

CHAPTER THREE.....................................35

CHAPTER FOUR 43

CHAPTER FIVE 51

CHAPTER SIX...60

CHAPTER SEVEN.....................................68

CHAPTER EIGHT 76

CHAPTER NINE......................................84

CHAPTER TEN 93

CHAPTER ELEVEN 102

CHAPTER TWELVE................................111

CHAPTER THIRTEEN 116

CHAPTER FOURTEEN 121

CHAPTER FIFTEEN 129

CHAPTER SIXTEEN 137

CHAPTER SEVENTEEN 144

CHAPTER EIGHTEEN 150

CHAPTER NINETEEN 164

CHAPTER TWENTY 173

CHAPTER TWENTY-ONE...................................184

CHAPTER TWENTY-TWO...................................196

CHAPTER TWENTY-THREE...............................205

CHAPTER TWENTY-FOUR 216

CHAPTER TWENTY-FIVE 223

CHAPTER TWENTY-SIX....................................233

CHAPTER TWENTY-SEVEN 242

CHAPTER TWENTY-EIGHT 250

CHAPTER TWENTY-NINE 260

CHAPTER THIRTY..268

CHAPTER THIRTY-ONE....................................277

CHAPTER THIRTY-TWO...................................285

CHAPTER THIRTY-THREE................................293

CHAPTER THIRTY-FOUR 300

CHAPTER THIRTY-FIVE 309

CHAPTER THIRTY-SIX 320

CHAPTER THIRTY-SEVEN 327

CHAPTER THIRTY-EIGHT 339

CHAPTER THIRTY-NINE 349

CHAPTER FORTY................................357

CHAPTER FORTY-ONE 366

CHAPTER FORTY-TWO........................375

CHAPTER FORTY-THREE....................383

CHAPTER FORTY-FOUR 394

CHAPTER FORTY-FIVE 402

CHAPTER FORTY-SIX..........................413

CHAPTER FORTY-SEVEN 423

CHAPTER FORTY-EIGHT 435

CHAPTER FORTY-NINE.......................443

CHAPTER FIFTY 451

CHAPTER FIFTY-ONE..........................464

CHAPTER FIFTY-TWO 474

ABOUT THE AUTHOR..........................480

A NOTE FROM THE AUTHOR 482

YA BOOKS BY JANICE SPINA - PG 13+ 484

OTHER MG/PT/YA BOOKS BY JANICE SPINA - 10+ 486

BOOKS BY J.E. SPINA FOR 15+ 490

BOOKS BY J.E. SPINA FOR 18+ 491

MAP OF NOELLA PROVINCE

CHARACTERS

Serena (16) - heroine of story, sister to Simon and Catalina

Simon (14) - brother of Serena and Catalina

Catalina (12) - sister of Serena and Simon

Solinara - Queen Fairy of Sovorotskina and mother of Serena and siblings

Gateskin - King Wizard of Sovorotskina and father of Serena and Siblings

Sovorotskina - Land of Goodness and Light, home of Serena and Family

Ressaphena - Goddess of Goodness and Light

Ramoforan- God of Goodness and Light

Noella - surviving child of Sovorotskina, during the capture of Taken Ones became Queen Fairy of Votovia

Sonovan - 1st King Wizard, husband of Noella, and ruler of Votovia

Noella II - descendant of Noella only child survivor of Legend of Taken Ones

Josoforan - King of Sovorotskina during capture of Taken Ones

Marolena - Queen Fairy of Sovorotskina during capture of Taken Ones

Hotenfaran - Wizard, uncle of Serena and siblings, brother of Queen Solinara

Procelina - Fairy, aunt of Serena and siblings

Arubane – adopted son of Procelina and Hotenfaran with many powers

Toleran - citizen guard of Sovorotskina

Miserva - citizen of Sovorotskina and wife of Toleran

Peteran - young son of Toleran & Miserva of Sovorotskina

Amora - Land of Faith and Love

Noderan - elder Amorans subject (Became King of Amora)

Davora – wife of Noderan (Became Queen of Amora)

Merlina - Land of Magic and Mystery

Merlinans - citizens of Merlina

Merona - Land of Myths and Legends

(Named after Fairy Princess captured by EO)

Meronans - citizens of Merona

Votovia - Land of Peace and Harmony

Votovians - peaceful but powerful subjects of Votovia

Savina - Queen Fairy of Votovia, present day ruler

Cavelan - King Wizard of Votovia, present day ruler

Adolphin - son of king and queen of Votovia

Anatonia Noella - daughter of king and queen of Votovia

Soneran - member of King Cavelan's guard

Latoran - member of King Cavelan's guard

Sprites - little tree people who lived in the forests around Sovorotskina and the other villages

Spindle - tree Sprite, friend of Serena's

Abason - tree Sprite, father of Spindle, Head Counsel of Sprites

Anabal - tree Sprite, mother of Spindle

Micah - brother of Abason, captured by Evil Ones

Parotovina - Land of Darkness and Evil, home of Evil Ones

Beregina - Queen Witch of Parotovina

Kaposkaran - King Wizard of Parotovina

Parotovinans - citizens of Parotovina

Quilarena - Goddess of Darkness and Evil

Quilottan - God of Darkness and Evil

Mitteran - Head Guard of scouting party of Parotovinans

Leanna - wife of Mitteran

Allonso (Al) - son of Mitteran & Leanna

Tessa- daughter of Mitteran & Leanna

Kelleran – Gatekeeper of Parotovina

Francia – wife of Kelleran

Botular – Eyes & ears of King Kaposkaran (HOH – becomes citizen of Sovorotskina)

Zuri - King of Merlina

Zuleima - Queen of Merlina

Zayleen - daughter of King Zuri/Queen Zuleima

Zukan - son of King Zuri/Queen Zuleima

Zuriann - daughter of King Zuri/Queen Zuleima

Cantok – large wolf from Unknown Territory – migrated to Sovorotskina

Notak – mate of Cantok

Tankor – male cub of Cantok

Rattor – male cub of Cantok

Maku – female cub of Cantok

Rabbinels – creatures created by Queen Solinara and Hotenfaran to feed the wolves and fulfill the need of the wolves to hunt and forage for food

Quintaroon – a creature created by the Wizards of Parotovina

Catlings – cat-like creatures that roam the UT

Animals in King Gateskin Barn – chickens, Milly the cow, Hank the horse

<u>Acronyms:</u>

EVIL ONES – EOs

TAKEN ONES – TOs

DESCENDANTS OF TOs – Ds

UNKNOWN TERRITORY – UT

Parotovinan Wizards – Head Wizard – Marno

Wizard #2 – Fortag

Wizard #3 – Wassor

Wizard #4 – Tornak

Wizard #5 – Kerno

Wizard #6 – Sufan

Parotovinans with powers –

Henno & Jenara – husband & wife

Danko – kind Parotovinan guard

Garita – wife of Danko

Harmony – daughter of Danko & Garita

Celdrick – son of Danko & Garita

Aneka – daughter of Danko & Garita

Dargonet – God of Dark Magic

Aharona – sister of Navaeha from Dragonaria

Callum – Aharona's dragon

Nevaeha – Aharona's sister

Evander – Navaeha's dragon

Isla and Marcellus – parents of
Aharona and Nevaeha and rulers of
island of Dragonaria – Land of
Dragons

Elowen – evil sister of Aharona and
Nevaeha

Jelitza – cousin of Aharona and
Navaeha

Verite – female dragon belonging to
Jelitza

Mianna – friend of Elowen

Matilda – cook on Dragonaria to King
Marcellus and Queen Isla

Madrigal – male dragon – lives in Sovorotskina – turquoise scales with turquoise eyes – kindly dragon

Izara – mate to Madrigal – lives in Sovorotskina – purple scales with purple eyes – cantankerous dragon

VILLAGES:

Sovorotskina – Land of Goodness & Light – King Gateskin/Queen Solinara

Parotovina – Land of Evil & Darkness King Kaposkaran/Queen Beregina

Votovia – Land of Magic & Mystery - King Cavelan/Queen Savina

Amora – Land of Faith & Love – King Noderan/Queen Davora

Merona – Land of Peace & Harmony – Ruled by Healers

Merlina – Land of Myths & Legends – King Zuri/Queen Zuleima

Dragonaria – Land of Dragons – island south of Novella Province – King Marcellus/Queen Isla

CHAPTER ONE

Spindle continued his rounds as Head Guard and flew around the forest surrounding Sovorotskina to inspect the area for any problems that may be coming their way.

He had heard the Quintaroons discussing something earlier that was quite disturbing to him while they were on their walk. He didn't like what he had heard from them. They were planning on reverting back to their creature states to see if they could flip back to being humans once again.

The Sprite was concerned for the safety of his good friend, Serena. Serena's siblings, Simon and Catalina, were seen walking behind the Quintaroons as their shadows to ensure the creatures behaved themselves. He did not trust these creatures not to create havoc everywhere they went.

Spindle would make sure there was a spell on the door of the creatures' house to keep them from getting loose. He planned on discussing this situation with King Gateskin as soon as he had completed his rounds over Sovorotskina.

As he was heading over to the King's house, he felt a wind pick up over his head which caused him to fly up to a high tree for a better vantage point. What he saw was a surprise.

Black clouds were seen coming his way. There were three dark shapes that became clearer the closer they came to him. Now he could distinguish what they were and flew down to meet them.

"What brings you back this way?" Spindle asked the visitors.

"Nice to see you too, Spindle," Jelitza stated with a frown.

"Aren't you happy to see us, Spindle?" Navaeha giggled as she looked at the Sprite's serious face.

"Sorry, I didn't mean to sound unwelcoming that way. Nice to see you all too."

"Leave him alone, you two. That is his job to find out why we are back. He is the Head Guard, after all," Aharona said as she winked at Spindle.

These visitors were from the island of Dragonaria, Land of the Dragons. They visited a few times in the past and even assisted the King and Queen with some problems they had in finding the lost Medallion. Aharona and Navaeha were sisters and Jelitza was their cousin. The two sisters trained dragons on their island and came on the backs of their dragons, Callum, Evander and Jelitza on Verite, to visit once again, but this time they had been invited to return at any time by King Gateskin.

The three dragons sniffed and licked the Sprite as he came closer to welcome them. Spindle wiped off the dragons' saliva and petted them on their wings.

"Nice to see you all again. I really didn't need a bath though, you know," he relayed to the happy dragons who were ready to lick him again from head to toe.

Turning to the three women he asked, "What brought you back this way?"

"There he goes again being so formal. I can't believe you, Spindle. We are friends, aren't we?" Jelitza said with impatience clearly in her voice.

"Well, I guess, sort of. We have met a few times now," he tried to explain.

"There. Now let's begin again, shall we?" Jelitza said, exasperated.

Spindle sighed and said, "Okay, please explain why you are here again."

"That is much better, Spindle," Jelitza guffawed.

"That is enough from you, young lady," Aharona said to stop the banter. "We need to see King Gateskin about an issue we have. I'm sure he will have a solution for us."

"Okay. I'll lead the way. Follow me," Spindle stated without looking at Jelitza who still wore a face of discontent. "But you must instruct your dragons to behave themselves while we are gone."

"Of course, we always do that," Navaeha stated as she pointed at Evander and said, "You heard the Head Guard. You need to behave yourselves. We will bring you back a reward if you do."

Evander snuffed out a puff of smoke in a ring as he nodded to his mistress, Callum and Verite. The three dragons quickly disappeared under their cloaks of invisibility and fell asleep.

CHAPTER TWO

King Gateskin was on alert when Spindle sent him a message through his mind that the dragon ladies were back.

Gateskin was waiting outside his house when they arrived. He greeted them warmly and invited them into his home where his wife was already preparing some refreshments.

Queen Solinara had not gotten along with the dragon ladies at their first meeting but now all that had transpired at that time was forgiven. It was just a misunderstanding, the ladies claimed, when they disrespected King Gateskin. They humbly apologized over and over to mollify the Queen who had been quite upset.

The Queen looked up at the visitors and smiled, shaking their hands in welcome and directing them to take a seat as she poured her special brew of tea and served them some fresh-baked raspberry scones.

"Did you leave your beautiful dragons in the woods?" Solinara inquired.

"Yes, they promised to behave, I assure you, Queen Solinara."

"Oh, I am not worried about that. I'm sure they will. I was hoping to see them before you leave. They take my breath away and I especially love Evander. He is quite a charmer."

Navaeha perked up at this and responded, "I am surprised that you said that, Queen Solinara. No one likes Evander after first meeting him."

"I wasn't too sure about him at my first meeting but we have met more than once now and I feel that he likes me too."

"I think he does. He may even fear you, Queen, because of your powers."

Queen Solinara chuckled at that. "I really don't think a dragon could ever fear me."

King Gateskin waited until the ladies were through exchanging banter and cleared his throat to get their attention, "Sorry to interrupt but is there a problem, ladies, that brought you back so soon?"

Aharona turned her attention back to the King. "Well, there is a little issue that we are trying to solve about lending you some dragons. Our father is not at all open to this. We tried to explain to him that you would not take advantage of the power you would have in your possession with two dragons. He fears that you would use them in a dangerous way against your enemies."

"I don't plan to use them like that, Aharona. You know that. You also know that I am a peace-loving man who would not harm anyone unless I had to protect my family and villagers."

"Oh, yes, I tried to explain all that to our father but he wouldn't budge. He is fearful also that if he gives you two dragons others would want some also. He cannot trust others to be kind and caring masters of these creatures."

"I see what you mean. I understand completely. I would feel the same way. It might be best if I meet with him privately to explain my reason for having two dragons on my land."

"Well, I…I don't know if he…," Aharona began.

"No worries I will fly there and he won't have to worry about traveling such a long distance."

Queen Solinara spoke to her husband's mind, "Are you crazy? Why would you do that? He could have you killed for going there. You won't know if he is dangerous."

"No worries, my dear. I can handle anything that comes my way."

"I hope so, Gateskin, but I will worry just the same."

"I know you will, my love. You always do." Gateskin winked at his wife and smiled to ease her worries.

Spindle stayed by the King's side and spoke to him the same way. "I will accompany you, my king, and do whatever you need me to do to protect you."

"Yes, of course, you will be by my side, Spindle. I wouldn't think of leaving without you and your valuable counsel. I will also take a few other guards with us for extra protection if we need it."

Spindle nodded in agreement but felt uneasy about the long journey and what they would have to face on this island, especially the dragon ladies' sister, Elowen, who used Dark Magic in the past when she last visited Sovorotskina. Spindle shivered at the thought of seeing her again. The evil surrounding her was intense and powerful.

CHAPTER THREE

The dragon ladies sighed in disappointment after the discussion was completed. They were unsuccessful in deterring King Gateskin from traveling to their island to speak with their father. They feared that nothing good would come out of this meeting.

Queen Solinara walked back with the ladies to see their dragons, or at least hear them, who were sound asleep and snoring quite noisily under their cloak of invisibility.

Aharona clapped her hands to awaken them and waited to see their expressions of surprise when Queen Solinara stepped forward to greet them.

"Look who is here to see you," Aharona exclaimed.

Evander stood up and bowed to the queen and poked Callum and Verite to do the same.

"It is a pleasure to see you again, Queen Solinara. You are looking quite beautiful as always," Evander delivered his most eloquent greeting.

Callum cleared his throat, nodded and responded, "Yes, you are quite fetching, my queen."

"I agree, Queen! You are quite fetching," Verite added.

"You are all so kind and gallant. I thank you for your kind words. You are all as spectacular as I remembered at our last meeting. What have you been up to?" The three dragons spread their wings to show off their colors that caught the light.

Callum's rainbow body sparkled as his green eyes glowed while Evander's blue, red and gold scales grew brighter and his blue eyes bluer.

Verite showed off her silver scales and blinked her silver eyes to get the Queen's attention.

Evander blushed at first but had to think about this for a minute. "Nothing much, Queen Solinara, other than the usual naps and flying around looking for something tasty to eat."

"Oh, that is right. I almost forgot. I brought you something that I think you will find very tasty." Queen Solinara smiled and whipped out of thin air three furry creatures that were plump enough to satisfy the hungry dragons.

"Ooh," the dragons exclaimed in delight as they reached forward to grasp a furry creature and proceeded to stuff them into their salivating jaws.

"I hope that was to your liking, Evander, Callum, and Verite," Solinara stated, with a pleased expression.

"Oh, yes. These creatures were very tasty!" Evander cried out in pleasure.

Callum nodded and wiped the feathers away from his mouth before responding, "My oh my, that was delicious! Where did you obtain such scrumptious creatures, Queen?"

"I agree, Queen, that was a tasty snack," Verite acknowledged.

"I have powers to do that to please special visitors like yourselves. After all, you helped us to find the lost Medallion. We never would have been able to do that ourselves."

"Not Verite, but it was our pleasure, Queen, to help you in any way we can. Can we do something else for you and King Gateskin? By the way, where is he?"

"Well, we may be asking you for your assistance again soon. In the meantime, don't worry about it. King Gateskin is preparing to travel to Dragonaria soon."

"What? He is coming to our island," Evander asked in surprise.

"Yes, he is meeting with your ruler, King Marcellus."

"Really, why?" Callum asked, curiously.

"You shouldn't be so inquisitive, dragons. This does not concern you," Navaeha scolded them.

"That is all right, Navaeha. I was the one to bring it up," Queen Solinara insisted.

"They don't need to know such things. They are entirely too meddlesome for their own good," Aharona stated, frowning at the dragons who bowed their heads in shame.

Jelitza kept quiet but nodded in agreement.

"Will you be escorting my husband to Dragonaria, ladies?"

"I think we should, Queen Solinara, for safety's sake. My father could send out some other dragons to intercept him if he came alone," Aharona states with a grim expression.

"Oh, no. My husband could be injured. Please keep him safe, ladies. I would be indebted to you if you could."

"That is our plan. We know how stubborn our father is. We will ensure the King's safety at all costs, I assure you, Queen," Navaeha responded.

"Thank you, both. I appreciate that. I am going to worry anyway but now I will feel better knowing that he is being watched over by all of you and your magnificent dragons."

The three dragons bowed their heads at the Queen and smiled as much as dragons could smile.

"Well, I had better get back to see how the King is doing in his preparations. I will have to provide some food for the journey for all of you."

"Please don't go into too much trouble, Queen. We are still full of your delicious scones and tea."

"No worries, Aharona and Navaeha, I always do this when my husband has to travel any distance. I want to make sure he keeps up his strength."

"He looks plenty strong to me," Navaeha responded as her cheeks flushed.

The King was tall and quite robust and muscular with his blonde hair, unruly at times, that swept off his forehead and brushed against his brows as he moved his head, and gorgeous blue eyes that would make any woman swoon as Navaeha just did.

"Yes, he is," Queen said with a giggle.

"We will wait here for the King. Let him know that, okay, Queen Solinara?"

"Of course, I'm sure he will be along shortly. Goodbye to all of you. Take care of yourselves and my husband, Spindle, and the other guards. I look forward to hearing that all goes well."

"I hope it does too, Queen," Aharona sighed, not too sure that things would work out.

CHAPTER FOUR

When Queen Solinara arrived back at their home she found her husband, Spindle, and guards gathered together in discussion.

"Is everything all right, dear?" Solinara asked.

"Yes, of course. I am just discussing what we will be doing when we arrive at Dragonaria. I want my men to be prepared for anything."

"I see. I spoke with the ladies and their dragons. They assured me that they would watch over all of you to ensure your safety."

"You didn't need to do that, my love. I assured you already that we will be safe."

"I know but I am your wife and it is my duty to make sure that you are safe."

Gateskin took his wife aside and gave her a hug and kiss and whispered, "I love you, Solinara. I will always return safely. I promise you. Can you do something for me? I want Serena to prepare a place for the dragons while we are gone?"

"Of course, I will. But are you sure? What if you can't get permission from the King?"

"I have a good feeling about this. Don't worry."

"Okay. Let me get some provisions for you and your men. I will be right back."

Spindle came to the door and called, "Queen, is Serena around?"

"Yes, she is in her room. I will call her for you, Spindle."

"Serena, Spindle is here to see you."

"I'll be right out."

Spindle shuffled his feet and waited as he kept looking down the corridor to Serena's room. His eyes grew wide when he spotted her.

"Oh, hi Spindle. I didn't expect to see you today. I thought you were on border patrol all day."

"Well, I was but now King Gateskin needs me to travel along with him."

"Travel? Where are you going?" Serena's voice raised in concern.

"We are traveling to Dragonaria to speak with King Marcellus."

"Really? That is a long way. How long will you be gone? Will you be safe?"

"I think so. We are bringing more guards with us and will be escorted by the dragons and the ladies."

"That's good to know. The ladies will make sure you are safe."

"I suppose so."

"Are you worried, Spindle?"

"Maybe a little."

"Serena took Spindle's hand in hers and held it as tightly as she could for a little Sprite and leaned down and planted a kiss on his brown cheek.

"What was that for, Serena?" Spindle said in a shocked voice.

"Just to keep you safe and also so that you would remember that I...I..."

"Love me?" Spindle responded with a grin.

"Maybe a little," Serena said and grinned back at him.

"Ditto."

"What?"

"You heard me. See you soon, Serena."

"Are you okay, Serena?" her mother asked when she saw Serena's flushed face.

"I'm...I'm fine, Mother."

"Come here and help me. I am preparing some food for the men. Help me put them into these baskets and bring them out to your father. He will be waiting for them."

"Okay, Mother." Serena walked out with the baskets and handed them to her father.

"Are you all right, Serena?" her father asked her when he saw her flushed face.

"I'm...I'm fine. Take care and watch over Spindle for me."

"I will, Serena. Don't worry. You and your mother worry too much. We will be okay and home before you miss us," Gateskin hugged and kissed his daughter and her siblings before he and his men, with Spindle pulling up the rear, headed out to meet the ladies and their dragons to begin their journey to Dragonaria.

Solinara waved and threw kisses to her husband and hugged her children who were looking a little nervous to see their father leaving on this long journey.

"They will all return soon, don't worry. I will get lunch started for us. You can feed the animals in the barn, pick some vegetables and feed the wolves. I'm sure they will be howling soon for their mid-day meal."

"Okay, Mother," Simon and Catalina responded and headed to the barn and the garden.

Serena nodded and went to feed the wolves who were pacing back and forth in front of their empty bowls. Her mind kept going back to Spindle who looked a little apprehensive about this journey. She wondered why. He never was upset about anything.

She went about scooping out the food for the wolves and thinking over the possible dangers that Spindle and her father could be facing. She shivered at the thought and said a silent prayer for their safety.

Queen Solinara spoke later with her children and told them, "Your father and I discussed this before he left. He wants you to build a lair for the dragons for when he returns. We are not sure if we will have the permission from King Marcellus or not but we need to be prepared in case we are successful in obtaining them. Do you think you and your siblings can manage to build such a place?"

"Of course, Mother. We will do our best to make it as large as possible and spacious too. We know how big they are. We will use a little magic along with the assistance of the guards to lift and bring the needed supplies to the area. We will build it far enough away from the house, barn and wolves huts."

"Yes, I was going to suggest that, Serena. I think you have this all figured out already. Well, after we eat, go make your plans with Simon, Catalina and the guards."

Solinara messaged the King about the lair that Serena was going to design. Gateskin was pleased to hear this.

CHAPTER FIVE

In Dragonaria Elowen could feel something coming their way. She went back to her house and conjured up some more of her new Dark Magic in case she needed to use it.

Mianna was hiding in the bushes near Elowen's hut and watched her enter and come out with a vial of blue liquid. She shivered to think that it was more of Elowen's Dark Magic. She couldn't believe how gullible she had been to be this woman's friend after what Elowen had done to endanger Noella Province with her Dark Magic.

She had heard how Elowen had caused havoc in Sovorotskina for King Gateskin when she tried to steal the chest with the Medallion from the King. Elowen was also feared on all of Dragonaria because of her powers. No one dared to venture close to her house.

She had to tell Aharona and Navaeha what Elowen was doing. She feared for her own life and the lives of all of Dragonaria if Elowen released any of this Dark Magic.

When she arrived at the two sister's huts, they were empty. She had to tell someone about Elowen. She headed toward the King's and Queen's palace to warn them of the dangers ahead. She had promised to keep an eye on Elowen for the King. He would expect her to keep him abreast of what his eldest daughter was now doing.

***

Aharona and Navaeha were in the lead of King Gateskin and his negotiating party as they headed toward Dragonaria. Aharona prayed that her father would be open to listening to King Gateskin's proposal to obtain two dragons without too much histrionics.

They had been traveling for a couple of hours now and had only taken a short rest and some refreshments that Queen Solinara had provided for them. The winds could be grueling and fierce as they traveled causing them to slow down and speed up again when they could, which made for a difficult journey at times even using some magic to help them along the way. But this magic did shorten the journey somewhat.

They were nearing Dragonaria now and Aharona could see the outline of the island through the clouds. It always took her breath away.

She nodded to Navaeha as they guided their dragons to the island near their parent's home. It was smaller from up here but grew in size the nearer they came. She always loved looking at it from the sky. It was so beautiful, lush and green, surrounded by the blue of the ocean, and serene, but soon would not be so.

Navaeha whispered to her, "Don't worry, Father will listen and eventually agree to allow them to have two dragons."

"Do you really believe that, Navaeha? Have you forgotten how stubborn Father can be?"

"I know, Aharona. But King Gateskin has a way with people and I think he will find a way to convince Father that he will treat the dragons kindly and take good care of them. He is a peace-loving man and would never use them in a warring manner."

"I know that, but Father doesn't, Navaeha!" Aharona stated, strongly. "Shh, be quiet now or the King will hear us."

King Gateskin had already tuned in to the sisters' conversation and heard every word. He would have to try harder to convince their father of his intentions for wanting two dragons. He would promise not to use them in any way to cause them or anyone else harm. He only hoped that it would not come down to using them against his enemies. His plan was to have them to keep away any warring ideas from anyone who threatened his people or his home and land.

Mianna looked up before she entered the house of the King and Queen. She called out to the visitors when no one was there to give her permission to enter. She saw two dragons and several others flying behind them heading her way.

She stepped aside as they all landed. The dragons were yawning and looking exhausted from the long journey. She waited for Aharona and Navaeha to come to her.

"What are you doing here, Mianna?" Aharona asked, clearly puzzled to see her.

"I was looking for you and Navaeha first but when you weren't home, I came here to see your parents with an urgent message."

"What message?" Navaeha queried.

"Well, you know that I am not a friend of your elder sister any longer. I had hoped that you and I could be friends again. I know I have not been a good friend when I sided with your sister, Elowen. I have to apologize again."

"I think you already did that, Mianna. We forgave you," Aharona stressed.

'I...I know, but I still feel bad about it all, especially now since your sister is...."

"Is what, Mianna? What are you trying to tell us?" Navaeha asked, with impatience.

"I'm sorry. I had wanted to share this with your father and mother too."

"Aren't they home?" Aharona asked.

"I don't know. I called out to them but no one answered. There are no guards around either."

Aharona exchanged worried glances with her sister and said, "Where could they be? There is always a guard or two around watching over the castle."

"That is strange. Maybe they had to leave to visit part of the island and took the guards with them," Navaeha explained.

"I don't like this. What did you want to share with our parents, Mianna?" Aharona insisted.

"Well, I saw Elowen leaving her hut with a vial of blue liquid. I fear that she has made more Dark Magic. I have seen this color liquid before. It could be quite dangerous. I don't know why she would need it. There are no problems here on the island."

"Oh no, we better warn King Gateskin," Aharona announced.

"Who is King Gateskin?" Mianna questioned as she looked at the others who were walking toward them.

Jelitza interjected, "He is a powerful and benevolent wizard king. That's who he is."

King Gateskin grinned at Jelitza's words of praise as he had overheard the interchange between the sisters, cousin, and the other young woman. He came up behind them and asked, "Is there a problem, ladies?"

"I'm afraid there is, King. It's our elder sister, Elowen. Of course you remember her." Aharona rolled her eyes and sighed.

"Yes, I do remember her. She is difficult to forget. What is she up to now?"

Navaeha began to explain, "Well, it appears that she has conjured up some more of her Dark Magic. She may have foreseen your arrival and is prepared to fight back."

Spindle flew and landed on the King's shoulder as he whispered in the King's ear, "Can I be of assistance, King?"

"Not yet, Spindle. Gather the men and we will have a little meeting to discuss what our next step will be."

"Yes, King, right away." Spindle flew back to the exhausted guards and gathered them together to meet with the King.

Before they could begin a discussion, a fierce wind picked up that increased in intensity and surrounded them in a black cloud.

CHAPTER SIX

The three dragons flew above the dark cloud and saw what was the cause of this wind. They surrounded Elowen and blew out their own smoke to blind and push her back from harming everyone below.

"What are you doing here, Elowen?" Callum asked in a gravelly voice.

"None of your business, dragon. Leave me alone and go on your way or I will have to…"

"What will you have to do, Elowen," Evander asked, as he grinned at her showing his teeth.

"Never mind. I will be back." Elowen turned in a huff and disappeared in a black cloud.

"I guess she didn't like your face, huh, Evander?" Verite laughed.

"Maybe it was yours, Verite!" Evander snapped.

The dragons flew back down to the group and announced, "She will not bother you anymore. Well, at least for the time being," Callum announced, proudly winking at Evander while Evander snarled at Verite. Verite grinned unaffected.

"Thank you, for coming to our rescue, Callum, Evander, and Verite," King Gateskin stated, as he conjured three fluffy creatures that were quickly devoured by the hungry and appreciative dragons.

The dragons licked their lips and spit out the feathers that stuck there. They bowed in thanks to the generous king and waited for word from their mistresses that they could go to their dens to rest.

Aharona, Navaeha and Jelitza nodded to their dragons and patted them on their heads. "It's time for you to rest. We are sure you are as tired as we are. Thank you for being so diligent in watching over us."

The dragons nodded and flew into the air and went back to their dens to catch up on some much-needed sleep.

King Gateskin said, "That is why I need at least two dragons. What they just did for us is worth more than words can express. Do you understand? I don't want to have a war or harm anyone. I want to keep my land, people, family and animals safe from harm from others who threaten us. That is all."

Aharona sighed, "Yes, we understand but you need to convince our father of this. He is not an easy person to reason with or even discuss something he refuses to believe."

"I can be stubborn too, Aharona, when I want something," King Gateskin stated, in a somber tone.

"Well, we need to find our father first before anything can be discussed," Aharona said.

"Yes, of course. My men need to rest before we have any discussions with your father. Is there somewhere we can get refreshments and rest?"

"Yes, of course. Please come into our parent's home. There are plenty of bedrooms. We will get some food for all of you. So sorry we forgot our manners. You were always so gracious as host and hostess to us on your land. Please forgive us," Navaeha said, with a bow.

"No problem, Navaeha. We appreciate your kindness and hospitality." Turning to Spindle and the other guards, King Gateskin said, "Come everyone. It is time to rest and get something to eat. Afterwards we will have our meeting with the King and Queen of Dragonaria."

They followed the two sisters, their cousin and friend inside the palatial home of the King Marcellus and Queen Isla. Everything was sparkling and highly polished. Two huge golden chandeliers graced the fifty-foot ceilings. Tall columns stood on each side of the grand hall with a split staircase at the center of the room, one staircase going to the left and the other to the right. Above on the second floor were long corridors and many doors leading to multiple rooms.

The sisters guided the group up to the rooms and got them settled. Aharona and her sister, their cousin, Jelitza and friend, Mianna went into the chef's kitchen to prepare something for their guests.

They looked around for the cook and housekeeper but no one was there. Where has everyone disappeared?

Aharona and Navaeha looked at each other and shrugged their shoulders. "This is very strange, Aharona. There is always someone here. They need to keep preparing food for our parents and keep the house in order. They never leave this early to retire."

"I know. I don't like this at all. Something must have happened to them. What are we going to do, Aharona?"

"Well, we need to feed our guests first. After we will get our dragons to fly us over the island so we can find them. They have to be somewhere."

"Okay. But what are we going to make for everyone? We don't know how to cook. The cook always did that for all of us. All I know is how to pick fruit and peel and eat it," Navaeha confided with an embarrassed look.

"Don't worry, you two. I can cook," Mianna stated with a grin.

"Who taught you to cook?" Aharona asked, with a frown.

"I can cook too," Jelitza announced, as she grinned in pleasure when she saw her cousins' surprise.

"You too? Who taught you to cook, Mianna?" Navaeha asked, clearly shocked.

"My grandmother taught me when I was little. I stayed with her while my mother was working in the fields," Mianna explained.

"What about you, Jelitza?"

"Well, my mother taught me. I learned how to do a lot on my own when she got sick."

"Oh, yes, I remember you took care of her until she passed. I'm sorry I forgot about that," Aharona stated, in a contrite voice.

"That's all right. I had no choice. My grandmother was already gone so there was no one else to take care of my mother."

"Our mother did help you from time to time and took you in until you decided to move out on your own," Aharona said.

"I know. I appreciated your mother's help."

"Well, enough talking. We need to prepare something for our hungry guests. They will want to eat once they have rested." Navaeha interrupted.

The four ladies gathered what they needed after Mianna and Jelitza instructed and began to prepare a meal fit for the King, his guards, and Henno and Jenara, powerful couple who migrated from Parotovina to Sovorotskina to escape the evil King Kaposkaran.

***

Down below the kitchen was a cellar or dungeon where the wine and other goods were kept so they would not spoil. Next to the wine racks were two cages. In those cages were the staff, guards, cook and the King and Queen of Dragonaria.

CHAPTER SEVEN

"Did you hear something, Marcellus? There is someone walking around in the kitchen."

"Yes, I think you're right, Isla. I hear them too. It sounds like our girls are home. Make a lot of noise and scream as loud as you can. All of you scream now!"

The King's staff began banging the bars of the cages and yelling as loud as they could until their voices were strained and hoarse.

Upstairs in the kitchen the four young women were making a lot of noise themselves shuffling around the pots and pans and cutting tools.

Jelitza suddenly stopped chopping and stood still. Her eyes grew wide as she cried out, "Listen everyone. Did you hear someone screaming? I think it came from the cellar."

"What? Maybe it's the staff. They may have gotten trapped down there. I'll go and check. You keep cooking," Aharona stated as she headed toward the cellar door. Navaeha followed closely behind her, listening.

"The door is stuck! Why would the door be stuck like this? I think it's locked. Do you know where the key is, Navaeha?"

"Yes, I saw Father put it in the drawer by the stove. It's way in the back."

"Well, go get it!" Aharona exclaimed in an impatient manner.

"I'm going. Maybe it's nothing. Why would they all be down there together anyway?"

"I don't know but we will soon find out if you will put the key into the hole."

"Patience, sister dear," Navaeha stated as she rolled her eyes.

They pulled open the old door and hurried down the stairs. They looked around and heard the voices screaming their names.

"Mother, Father! What are you doing here? Who put you down here?" Aharona asked, clearly puzzled.

"Never mind asking questions, just get us out of here," King Marcellus exclaimed, his face beet red from screaming.

"Are you all right?" Navaeha asked as she gave her parents a hug.

"Your father will explain, but first I think he wants to get the persons responsible for this," her mother declared, her face covered with perspiration.

"Get the others out too, Aharona," her father commanded.

"Is everyone okay?" Aharona asked as she helped everyone out of the crowded cage.

"I guess we are, but the people responsible will not be soon," one of the King's guards stated.

The King nearly took the stairs by threes to get out of the cellar with his guards close behind him. The guards looked ready and able to do the King's bidding.

Aharona and Navaeha moved out of the way as everyone hurried past them, happy to be out of their confinements.

When the cook and housekeeper came into the kitchen, they were shocked to see Jelitza and Mianna cooking.

"What are you doing in my kitchen?" the cook announced, with a frown of displeasure.

"Oh, there you are, Matilda. We wondered where you had disappeared to. We are preparing a meal for our honored guests," Jelitza explained.

"Guests? We have guests? I was not told of any guests?" Matilda bristled at this announcement.

"Who are our guests?" Queen Isla asked.

Aharona and Navaeha exchanged worried glances before Aharona began to explain. "Sorry, Mother. We escorted King Gateskin, and his guards to meet with Father. Where did Father disappear to now?"

"He has a mission. He will explain later. Let's discuss this after our guests leave. No reason to involve them."

"All right, but King Gateskin may be able to help you find out who did this to you," Navaeha stressed.

"No, I do not want to talk about it now. Take care of your guests," Queen Isla stated in a strong voice.

"We need to feed our guests, Mother. Can we have the cook and housekeeper help us?" Aharona asked.

"I don't see why not." Queen Isla turned to her cook to instruct her, "Matilda, please help the girls cook up a meal for our guests."

"Yes, Queen Isla, right away." Matilda put her apron on and hurried to take over the cooking from the ladies.

"We put our guests in rooms upstairs, Mother. We will need the housekeeper to clean their rooms and bathrooms after they come down to eat," Navaeha stressed.

"Of course, that will be taken care of, dear." The Queen nodded to the housekeeper who moved quickly away to do her job.

"Now are you going to tell me about our guests and why they are here?"

Aharona stepped closer to her mother and explained, "We wanted to talk to Father about loaning two dragons to King Gateskin. The King wants to take care of them and will never use them as weapons or cause anyone harm."

"Did you ask your father about this already?"

"Well, we did speak with Father about this previously," Aharona replied.

"What did he say?"

"Mother, you know what he would say. Maybe you can help us convince him that this is a good idea?"

"Aharona, I can't do that. Your father has his own mind and I cannot change it. What makes you think it is a good idea? Besides, now may not be the best time to ask him about this. He is still upset about what happened."

"I understand, Mother. Maybe if we wait a little bit before we ask him. I will have to explain all this to King Gateskin."

"Yes, that may be better to wait," her mother said with a deep sigh.

"I'd like to know who did this to you and father. But about the dragons, I know King Gateskin and have seen what a good leader he is and how he takes care of his family and land. Our dragons love him and his family. They are excellent judges of character of people and whether they are kind and caring."

"I understand that you believe this wholeheartedly, Aharona. You would not be able to find anything wrong with your dragons."

"They are honest, Mother. They are not afraid to tell us if we are wrong. We trust them, don't we, Navaeha?"

"Most definitely," Navaeha agreed.

Voices were heard coming from the upper floors as their guests came down ready for refreshments.

CHAPTER EIGHT

King Gateskin led his men into the dining room where tantalizing smells were emanating from the kitchen. He stopped abruptly when he saw the ladies and their mother, Queen Isla, in deep conversation. The subject was most likely about him and his men and the reason they came.

Aharona stopped talking when she spotted King Gateskin and his entourage. She left her mother's side and went to speak with the King.

"I hope you are rested, King Gateskin, and are hungry. Our chef and my cousin and friend have prepared a wonderful meal for you and your men."

"Yes, we are. Thank you, Aharona."

"Please let me introduce you to my mother, Queen Isla. Mother, this is King Gateskin of Noella Province."

"It is a pleasure to meet you, Queen Isla. I hope you will excuse our intrusion."

"It is nice to meet you too, King Gateskin. My daughters have been praising you and your kindness toward them when they visited your land. It is the least I can do to thank you for hosting them a couple of times."

"No problem at all. We have enjoyed their visits and their incredible dragons. That is why I am here to meet with your husband, King Marcellus. Is he available to meet with us now?"

"No, I'm afraid there is a problem that he is dealing with at the moment. He will return later. I do not know when that will be, unfortunately."

"Hmm, I see. Well, we can wait for a while. I must say that I could smell the food as we came down the stairs. It smells wonderful! I hope your chef and the others did not work too hard to prepare this meal. We do appreciate their efforts, I assure you."

The chef turned toward King Gateskin's voice and harumphed a few times but never met the King's eye.

Aharona laughed this off and shrugged her shoulders. "Our chef is very touchy about someone using her kitchen. She considers this her domain and no one should try to take it over. My cousin, Jelitza and friend, Mianna, did try to prepare a meal for you in her absence."

"I see. I can understand how she feels. I wouldn't want anyone to try to take over my position either." King Gateskin smiled and winked at the chef when she turned to look at him. Her face became flushed as she tried to hold back a grin at his remarks.

Navaeha giggled at this exchange. "Well, I think you may have made a friend, King Gateskin. Matilda never smiles at anyone."

"Well, I am honored to meet you, Matilda. I'm sure your food will be fabulous."

This caused Matilda to clear her throat and hang her head to hide the wide smile she was now wearing.

Spindle told the men to take a seat where there were place settings that the housekeeper had just put down.

Matilda directed Jelitza and Mianna to carry the food to the table and serve the men since they had invaded her kitchen. She planned to keep them busy also cleaning up the mess that they had managed to make before she came to rescue them.

The men stated their delight over what was being served. There were dumplings in a chicken broth, lamb chops with roasted potatoes, mixed vegetables and fresh baked loaves of bread.

They ate heartily and sat back to rest. For dessert Matilda had brought over some chocolate pudding and two apple pies she had prepared earlier in the day.

King Gateskin wiped his mouth after the last bite of pie and sat back with a satisfied sigh. Directing his remarks to the chef he said, "Well, this was a remarkable meal, Matilda. You are an excellent cook. If I could, I would lure you away from the King and Queen."

Matilda blushed and nodded her head before responding, "I thank you, King Gateskin, for your kind words. I appreciate that you enjoyed my cooking but I would never even think about leaving my homeland of Dragonaria and King Marcellus and Queen Isla."

Queen Isla grinned, "I'm happy to hear that, Matilda."

Matilda bowed to her queen and went back to putting the leftover food away.

Spindle whispered to the King, "Do you want us to look for King Marcellus?"

"No, we will wait."

Spindle nodded and sat on the King's shoulder to wait for his next command.

Queen Isla was fascinated by the Sprite who seemed to have the ear of King Gateskin. "Excuse me, King Gateskin. I haven't been introduced to this delightful… I'm not sure what he is."

"Oh, sorry, Queen Isla. This is my Head Guard, Spindle. He is a tree Sprite who lives in our forests on Noella Province. There are many Sprites there."

"I see. It is nice to meet you, Spindle. You are quite a dashing Sprite, may I say?" the Queen responded as she shook his little brown hand.

"It is my pleasure, Queen Isla, to meet you." Spindle bowed to the Queen.

The Queen smiled at Spindle and turned to Navaeha who waved at her to come to the back of the room. "Mother, do you want me to ask King Gateskin for assistance in finding who locked you, Father, and the others in the cages?"

"No, I don't want to involve our visitors in this. I already told your sister that. Your father is taking care of it."

"But who did this to you?" Navaeha asked, concern shadowing her face.

"I...I don't want to share this right now."

"But, Mother, if you know who did it, why don't you tell us? Was it Elowen?"

"I...I don't know for sure. There were three men in dark clothes and their faces were covered in masks. They ordered us to go downstairs. They held swords in their hands."

"Oh, Mother. That must have been frightening."

"Yes, it was. They never told us why."

"Do you think they wanted to steal from you?"

Aharona came over to see what her sister Navaeha was discussing that was upsetting their mother. She knew that her mother was still shaken over what had transpired earlier. It wasn't fair to push her to do anything about convincing father about the dragons. This wasn't the time.

They would have to wait for their father to return.

CHAPTER NINE

"What's going on, Navaeha?"

"Mother is upset over what happened but won't tell me who did it," Navaeha explained. "I think she knows or at least suspects that Elowen had something to do with it."

"Are you all right, Mother?" Aharona asked, disturbed by her mother's sudden tears.

Their mother shook her head and covered her face with her hands.

King Gateskin watched the exchange between the sisters and their mother. He got up from the table and walked over to them to see what was upsetting the Queen.

"Can I be of assistance, Queen Isla? Are you all right? I hope we haven't upset you in any way."

"Oh, no, of course not, King Gateskin. This has nothing to do with you and your men. We had an issue before you arrived and my husband is trying to settle it now."

"Is there anything that my men and I can do to help you?"

Before the Queen could respond, Navaeha and Aharona took King Gateskin aside to explain.

Navaeha began, "While you and your men were resting, we could not find our parents or the staff anywhere until we heard them calling from the cellar."

Aharona continued, "We went down to investigate and found our parents, staff and guards locked in cages there."

"Locked in cages?" King Gateskin repeated, clearly shocked.

"Yes, they do not know who did this to them, except that our mother said there were three masked men with weapons who forced them into the cages before leaving them there. I don't know how long they were there or who these men could be," Navaeha stated.

"Can I speak to your mother now?" the King asked, calmly.

"Of course, that is if Mother will tell you anything. She is quite upset and I think it is just hitting her now."

"I understand. Let me try to speak with her."

The sisters nodded and let King Gateskin walk over to their mother who was still crying.

"I'm sorry to disturb you, Queen. Your daughters told me what happened to you. I would like to assist you in finding out who did this to you and your husband and staff."

"I…I…don't know what to do. I fear for my husband's life. The men warned us to not tell anyone about them or they would …." Queen Isla's tears continued, stronger now.

Handing the Queen a handkerchief that he pulled out of mid-air, he waited until she had wiped her eyes and composed herself.

"I don't want to say this, but do you think your daughter, Elowen, is part of this?"

"I…I fear she may be. She has become deeper into Dark Magic, more than ever before. I think it is taking her over completely. I don't know my own daughter anymore. She has been high strung and belligerent since her teens. She always wanted to do her own thing and have her own way."

"I see. Where does she live?"

"She has had her own place since she was in her late teens. We couldn't keep her here because she was disruptive to her younger sisters. She moved out and hasn't visited much since unless she wants to cause trouble again."

"Why would she do this to you?"

"I don't know. She must have plans to take over the castle and control of the island."

"Where did your husband go?"

"He may have gone to her house to speak with her and find out what she wants from us."

"Let me help you. Please tell me where I can find Elowen's place."

The Queen called her daughters over. "Girls, King Gateskin wants to go to Elowen's house. Can you take him there and please be careful? Stay out of her way."

"Of course, Mother. We are happy to help in any way we can. As for staying out of her way, we can manage that very well with the help of our dragons. You know how Elowen fears our dragons," Aharona snickered.

The sisters led the King, Spindle, and the guards out of the castle and gathered outside to discuss where they were going. The sisters whistled for their dragons who flew to their side a few seconds later in a gust of wind.

Callum and Evander bowed to them and waited for instructions where they were going.

Aharona and Navaeha spoke to their dragons and explained where they wanted to take King Gateskin, Spindle and the guards.

"What is she up to now, Aharona?" Callum whispered.

"We don't know yet. We need to go there and rescue our father," she explained, and relayed what has transpired to cause this trip.

"Elowen is asking for trouble, isn't she?" Evander asked after listening to Navaeha's explanation.

"Isn't she always?" Navaeha grumbled, in discontent.

Turning to King Gateskin and his entourage, she asked, "Are you ready to follow us? Elowen's house is located on the other side of the island in a secluded area. I'm sure she will be prepared for anyone who tries to venture too close to her property. I only hope that Father is not in any danger. He did bring several of his guards with him. They traveled by foot with Father in a cart they pulled along."

"I think Father will be careful, Navaeha. He knows his daughter, along with all her tricks."

"But, Aharona, he doesn't know Dark Magic. How can he fight that? How can we?"

"Let us worry about that when we get there, ladies. Okay?" King Gateskin responded.

"I guess so," Navaeha replied, in a worried tone.

"Don't forget, you have two marvelous dragons with powers that can counterattack Elowen's.

Didn't you share with me that she is afraid of them?" King Gateskin continued.

"Well, yes, we did. But who knows what she has conjured up since the last time we had to deal with her," Navaeha stressed.

"We need to be ready for whatever she tries to do to deter us from getting too close. She can never be trusted," Aharona stated, grimly.

"Yes, sadly, we have learned this after many times she tried to harm us as we were growing up. Thank goodness for our dragons who were always there to protect us as they will do now," Navaeha said, with a shiver.

The group was ready to leave when Jelitza and Mianna came running out of the castle. "Do you want us to go with you, Aharona?"

"No, please stay here with my mother. She is quite upset and will need someone close by until we return."

"Okay, we can do that. We need to get out of the kitchen before Matilda wears us out!"

Aharona smirked, "Thank you, both. See you later."

The two young women waved goodbye as they stood watching the group leave.

Callum and Evander nodded in agreement to their mistresses' orders as they flew on their way with King Gateskin and company close behind.

CHAPTER TEN

King Marcellus and his guards moved stealthily around Elowen's hut which was now a larger house. She had added on space to make room for all her Dark Magic.

The King whispered to his men, "Be on the alert. She can be quite tricky and dangerous. Don't trust her if she comes out to speak with you. Stand far away and wait for my orders."

The men nodded as they warily looked around for this dangerous woman the King called his daughter.

A wind suddenly picked up around them causing them to fall over and grasp for something to hold onto. King Marcellus called out, "Elowen, stop this right now! I am here to speak with you."

Elowen raised her hands and lowered the wind as she stepped out of her house and looked at her father who was trying to get up from the ground as well as his men. "What do you want, Father?"

"I think you know, Elowen. You were behind those masked men who put us in the cages."

"I don't know what you speak of, Father. I would not do such a thing."

"If you didn't do that, who did?"

"I wouldn't know anything about that. Maybe you have enemies."

"I do not have any enemies, daughter."

"I wouldn't say that, Father. You and I know that you have at least one."

"Who would that be?"

Laughing, Elowen responded, "You are looking at her. Don't you know that we are enemies?"

"What are you saying?" her father asked, shocked and dismayed at her words.

"We have not been a family for a very long time since you kicked me out of your castle. Don't you remember?"

"I did not kick you out, Elowen. You refused to follow our rules if you lived there and you also tormented your younger sisters. I could not tolerate that."

"Well, you kicked me out of your palace to protect your precious little ones? Is that it? I was not important to you and never was."

"Why do you think that way? I love all of you and always have. But you have given me much grief that I have tried to overcome. You don't make things easy for me, Elowen. Why do you fight us? We are your family. We love you and want you in our lives but without Dark Magic."

"That will never happen, Father. I need my Dark Magic. It is the only thing that protects me and makes me feel loved. Something you never could do. You always favored my little sisters."

The King sighed heavily and shook his head at her words. "If you did not do this to us, who do you think did?"

"I don't know, Father, and don't care. Please leave my place now. You are not wanted here."

The King motioned to his men to leave while he watched his daughter go inside her house. He tried to keep his emotions in check as he turned away. What could he tell his wife? Who was responsible if Elowen wasn't?

Aharona and Navaeha looked down and saw their father and his guards moving away from Elowen's house. Where were they going?

"King Gateskin, look. There's my father and his guards. They are leaving. I wonder what happened," Aharona motioned.

"Maybe we should go down and find out, Aharona. Look at Father. He is upset. His face is all flushed and he is wiping his eyes. Is he crying? What happened here?"

Aharona instructed Callum to fly down near her father so she could hop off his back. When she was settled down on the ground, she called out to her father who was a short distance away now, "Father, wait a minute. What happened?"

"Aharona, what are you doing here? You better leave before your sister sees you."

"Why? What is she going to do? Has she hurt you?"

"No, not physically, but emotionally, yes. She said she had nothing to do with those men who locked us up."

"Really? She told you that. I don't believe it for a minute. Do you believe her?"

"I don't know what to believe. All I know is that she hates me and doesn't consider me her father anymore."

"What? Did she tell you that?"

"Yes, she did in so many words. I must get back to your mother now. I'm sure she would want to know what transpired and that I am not injured."

"That is why we are here to help you. Navaeha and I feared that Elowen would hurt you in some way. She is so unpredictable."

"Yes, she is. But I didn't expect her to be so belligerent. I have lost my oldest daughter for good. This Dark Magic has taken over her body, heart and soul completely. It's so sad."

"Please, Father, let me talk to her. You should go home. Mother is quite upset and needs you. We will take care of Elowen, don't worry."

"NO! You cannot do this! She will hurt you or even try to kill you. I don't want to lose both of you too. I couldn't bear it!"

"We are not alone, Father. We brought King Gateskin, Spindle, his Head Guard, and the other guards with us. Don't forget we have our dragons here to protect us. They won't let anything happen to us."

"Please be careful. I need to find out who is responsible for what they did to us and why. Come back to see me when you are finished speaking with your sister; that is, if she will see you at all."

"I think she will. Don't worry. Go home now. Okay?"

"Keep Callum close to you, Aharona. Okay? I love you."

"Of course, Father. He is always close to me. I love you too." Aharona was shocked at her father's words of endearment. He never really said that. Well, at least not for a long time since she was a little girl.

Navaeha, King Gateskin and his guards dropped down next to Aharona as King Marcellus and his guards marched away with the King in the cart.

"What did Father say, Aharona?"

"I am still in shock. He is quite distressed over her attitude. Can you imagine that she doesn't recognize him as her father anymore? Elowen hates him. I can't believe she said that to him! How awful! I know that he is not a soft, mushy father but he has always been there for us. Shame on her! Wow, she is heartless! Poor Father. It must be Dark Magic speaking for her."

"That's awful of her to say such a thing," Navaeha stressed, in disappointment. "I agree, it must be Dark Magic."

"That is what Father said. He thinks it has taken over Elowen's body, heart and soul."

King Gateskin stood at a distance but could still hear the sisters' conversation.

Watching them from her window, Elowen worked up a spell to stop them from coming any closer to her house.

CHAPTER ELEVEN

"Can I be of any assistance, ladies?" King Gateskin ventured closer to them once their conversation came to a halt.

Aharona cleared her throat and turned to face the King. "Father said Elowen did not lock them up. Someone else is responsible."

"I see. Do you believe that?"

Navaeha exchanged worried glances with her sister and answered, "I think she is responsible or at least through her Dark Magic. She could have made someone else do that just to spite our parents. She can be cruel at times like this."

"I don't think we are going to get her to talk to us. I feel Dark Magic around us. I can't move any closer to her house. Do you feel it too?"

"Yes, I do. Maybe it's time we return home too and make sure Father and Mother are all right."

"I am worried about Father. I have never seen him like this. He even said he loved me."

"What? He told you he loved you? He hasn't said that since we were little kids."

"I know, that's what I was thinking, Navaeha."

King Gateskin sent a message to Spindle who in turn corresponded with the guards, "We need to move away from here and return to see King Marcellus."

"We are ready to return when you are, ladies," King Gateskin announced. He could feel the cold emanating all around them. It was Dark Magic which could harm them if they stayed any longer. It was evident that Elowen did not want them there.

Aharona and Navaeha hopped onto their dragons and led the way back to their parent's home.

King Marcellus arrived back at his castle a short time before his daughters did. He went to see his wife right away to report what had transpired with their eldest daughter.

"What? She said that you are now enemies?" Queen Isla asked in shock. "If she didn't do it, who did?"

"I don't know. Nothing Elowen does lately shocks me. She is entirely under the influence of her Dark Magic. I think we have lost her, Isla." He covered his face in his hands as he shook in defeat.

"Please, dear. Don't give up yet. We will get her back. Did you see our younger daughters and King Gateskin and company?"

"I saw them behind us. I think they were leaving too. No one could get through that Dark Magic. It was making me and my men sick the longer we stayed."

"King Gateskin is here to speak with you. Did you know that?"

"Is he now?" King Marcellus humphed.

"Do you know what he wants?"

"Yes, I do and he will not get it!"

"What is the harm in letting him have two dragons? He seems to be kind and caring with Callum and Evander. They love him."

"Ha, those dragons would love anyone who feeds them!"

"Well, I guess, but I don't think that is all. They appear to admire him."

"What is there to admire?"

"He is quite good-looking. That is not all. He is polite with and supportive of our daughters, besides being strong, courageous, and intelligent."

King Marcellus looked at his wife with a frown. "Is that all?"

"These are essential qualities of a good king. They are the characteristics of you too, my dear." Queen Isla buttered up her husband after seeing the disgruntled look he had displayed hearing her words of praise of another man.

She put her arms around her husband and gave him a hug and a kiss to seal her words and make him feel better. It appeared to help prepare him for when King Gateskin came back.

They pulled apart when they heard their daughters' voices and that of King Gateskin as they entered the foyer.

"Are you all okay?" Queen Isla inquired as she looked her daughters over carefully.

"Yes, Mother, we are all fine. I'm sure Father filled you in on Elowen's latest tactics," Navaeha responded.

"I am sorry to hear that she did not welcome you into her home. I don't know what we are going to do with her. But I will not give up on getting her back."

"I don't know what we are going to do with her either, Mother. I fear it may be too late," Aharona sighed.

"Where is Father going?" Navaeha asked, as she watched her father walk away from them.

"He is distraught over Elowen," Queen Isla responded, sadly.

"We need him here now. King Gateskin wants to speak with him about the dragons," Aharona stressed, following closely behind her father.

King Gateskin stepped forward and stated, "If this is not an appropriate time to speak with the King, I can wait or come back later."

Queen Isla sighed heavily and said, "No, I will get him for you. Wait here."

King Gateskin watched the Queen almost run after her daughter and husband to catch them.

She tapped her daughter on the back and told her, "I will take care of him. He will come back to speak with King Gateskin. Go back to your guests and get them something to drink. It won't be long."

Aharona turned and headed to the kitchen where Matilda was cleaning up her domain and making it once again pristine with Jelitza and Mianna as her helpers.

"Can I get some tea or coffee for our guests, Matilda?"

"I will do that for you, Princess. My kitchen is once again mine and clean. You girls can leave now before you do any more damage here," she huffed, pushing the two out of the way to get to the coffee and tea pots.

"I guess we are not wanted anymore, Mianna. Let's get out of here before she finds something else for us to clean," Jelitza giggled.

Aharona tried not to laugh and instead smiled broadly at her cousin and friend.

"I am going to see my dragon. Verite is probably wondering why I haven't been by to see her for a while."

"Can I come?" Mianna asked, following behind her.

"Sure. Verite likes you, especially if you bring some of that sweet clover she loves."

"I will do that," Mianna responded and rushed out to get some. After that they headed to Jelitza's home a short distance away from the Palace.

***

"Your kitchen looks great, Matilda. Thank you for the coffee and tea. Ooh, you included some of your tasty ginger cookies. The men will love them as much as I do," Navaeha remarked, in gratitude.

"They are our guests, after all. I will take it to them. You needn't do that, Princess."

"Okay. I will go ahead and tell them to sit and enjoy them while we wait for my father to return."

CHAPTER TWELVE

King Marcellus returned with his wife to meet with King Gateskin and his men. Queen Isla had convinced her husband to keep an open mind and give King Gateskin a chance with two dragons.

King Gateskin and his entourage were enjoying the coffee, tea and cookies when they looked up to see the King and Queen coming into the large great room.

They rose and greeted the King and Queen and were instructed to sit down and relax. The King waved at Matilda, "Coffee please."

"Right away, King Marcellus." She bowed out of the room and returned with a pot of coffee and cookies for the King to share with the Queen.

King Gateskin waited for King Marcellus to begin their conversation. He sipped his coffee and kept his eyes on King Marcellus.

"I know why you are here, King Gateskin. My daughters filled me in after their last trip to Noella Province."

"I see," King Gateskin stated and waited.

"I have given this much thought about what you desire from my island and from me."

"Yes," King Gateskin, held his breath as he waited for King Marcellus to continue.

"I have decided to allow you to take two dragons on a trial basis. My daughters will go along with you and the dragons. Once the dragons have been trained to respond to you satisfactorily, you can keep them for two weeks. After that, my daughters will report back to me whether they are working out sufficiently to live safely there with you."

"I appreciate your confidence in allowing me to take them. I will do all I can to ensure their safety and wellbeing."

"I am happy to hear that, King Gateskin. I wouldn't have it any other way."

"Thank you, King Marcellus. I appreciate your generosity and kindness."

Aharona and Navaeha couldn't contain their surprise and delight over their father's decision. They cried out, "Thank you, Father!"

"You shouldn't be too excited just yet. It may not work out at all, daughters. You will be the ones to choose the appropriate dragons and train them to listen to King Gateskin and adjust to living in a different place altogether. It will not be as warm as this island is and quite different."

"We will do our best, Father," Aharona interjected as she exchanged smiles with her sister.

"Yes, we will, Father. We will work hard to make this happen."

King Gateskin waited for King Marcellus to rise and take leave before getting up along with Spindle and his men.

"I can't thank you enough, Queen Isla, for your intercessions. I know you had much to do to influence your husband. I assure you that the dragons will adjust to our land and new home. I will make sure everything is perfect."

"I pray that you do that, King Gateskin. My husband is not a forgiving man if things don't work out."

King Gateskin shook the Queen's outstretched hand and turned to Aharona and Navaeha for what would be the next step.

"Well, I guess it's time we visited the dragons and decided which ones to give to you, King Gateskin." Aharona explained.

CHAPTER THIRTEEN

King Gateskin gathered Spindle and the other guards and instructed them to follow the two dragon ladies to the dragons' den.

The men looked up in dismay when they heard this. "Will it be safe for us to go there?" one guard asked, dismayed.

Spindle took the frightened guard aside and scolded him, "Don't you think that the King knows the dangers and will keep us all safe. He would not lead you into danger."

"Um, I see. Okay. I'm sorry for asking, Spindle. Please forgive me."

Spindle whispered to Gateskin, "We will have to consider whether this man is suitable to be one of your guards."

"Yes, I agree with you, Spindle. But let's not be too hasty. He may turn around and show his bravery soon."

"Whatever you say, King. I will do your bidding." Spindle bowed to the King and flew up to his shoulder as they headed toward the dragons' den with the rest of the guards close behind.

As they neared the area where the dragons hung out, they noticed the multitude of dragons and the brilliant colors of their scales that shone in the sunlight overlooking the mountainous area causing a rainbow effect.

The dragon ladies, Aharona and her sister, Navaeha, turned to King Gateskin and instructed him to wait at a distance so as not to startle the dragons who were sleeping.

Aharona turned to her sister and spoke softly, "I think I know which ones to choose. Look over there at the pair that are sleeping close together. They have been inseparable since they were born. They would be perfect to go together."

"I agree, Aharona. They would support one another and keep each other company. I think they would be good listeners and adjust quickly to a new master such as King Gateskin."

"We need to wake them carefully. They can be cantankerous if disturbed too harshly, Navaeha."

"Of course. We better prepare the King and his men to back away and stay behind the trees over there until we can speak to the dragons through Callum and Evander."

King Gateskin was listening to their conversation and began to back away, pushing his men along with him and Spindle.

When the ladies turned, they saw the King and his men behind the trees.

"Do you think he heard us or maybe sensed that he needed to move back on his own, Aharona?"

"Hmm, could be that he heard us. We know how powerful he is. This is another one of his powers to hear even a whisper from a distance."

"Let me have Callum nudge them and begin an explanation of what we want from them."

"I think I will back away too, Aharona."

"Good idea. I don't blame you. We cannot be sure that they will cooperate at all. They may be settled in their life here and don't want to go elsewhere."

"We will find out soon enough, Aharona."

The ladies and the King and his guards watched silently as the two dragons were awakened by Callum and Evander.

A loud screeching was heard as each dragon woke up and looked around to see who was disturbing them from their nap.

Callum stepped closer to the smaller of the two dragons and said, "Sorry to wake you but it is of the utmost importance that you listen to our mistresses who have some exciting news to share with you."

"What? What news?" the smaller dragon asked, looking around to see where the mistresses were.

Aharona and Navaeha stepped forward as they held onto the wings of their dragons for safety and security.

CHAPTER FOURTEEN

The two awakened dragons bowed as the two sisters came closer.

"It is a pleasure to meet you both," Aharona announced after seeing them bow to her and her sister.

"Yes, it is a pleasure," Navaeha seconded.

"No, it is our pleasure, Princesses, to meet you," the male dragon announced.

"We would like to present you with a proposal from King Marcellus, our father."

"We're listening, Princess."

"First of all, please introduce yourselves. We don't know your names. There are so many of you and we have not been here to visit for a while," Aharona said.

"Of course, Princess. I am Madrigal and this is my mate, Izara."

"You are mated?" Navaeha asked in surprise.

"Yes, is that a problem?" Madrigal asked, swiveling his head around to look at Navaeha.

Navaeha moved back a little behind Evander who put his wing over her and met Madrigal with a warning look.

"I do not intend to harm you, Princess. Sorry about my tone of voice," Madrigal stated, bowing his head.

"That's better. Do you want to hear what King Marcellus has proposed?"

"Of course, please continue, Princess."

Aharona explained in detail what her father had said about the two dragons going to live on another land with a new King.

"Why are we doing this, Princess?" Madrigal inquired.

"Well, maybe I should introduce you to King Gateskin who will be the new master for both of you."

King Gateskin stepped forward and greeted the dragons in a flourish with hands extended filled with two fluffy creatures that caused the dragons to drool at the sight of these delicious treats.

"Please take these offerings, Madrigal and Izara. It is an extreme pleasure to meet you both. I look forward to getting to know you better."

Izara moved closer to sniff the creatures and waited for Madrigal to take one first.

Madrigal and Izara gripped a creature in their claws and stuffed them inside their drooling jaws where the creatures quickly disappeared.

They spit out the feathers that could not be digested and burped in delight as their faces showed their pleasure in wide grins which were directed at King Gateskin.

"Well, it looks like you won them over, King Gateskin," Aharona giggled.

"No doubt about that," Navaeha added with a chuckle.

"I am honored that you are both pleased with my offerings, Madrigal and Izara," King Gateskin stated as he extended his hands in greeting to pet the dragons' heads.

"It is our pleasure, King Gateskin, to meet you and enjoy these generous and delicious treats," Madrigal said with a bow.

"I look forward to learning more about this arrangement, Princesses," Izara spoke up in curiosity.

"I hoped you would," Aharona sighed in relief.

She explained that the land they were going to would not be as warm as Dragonaria and that it was heavily forested and had a larger population of people than their present home.

"Hmm, I see. Do I understand that you would be training us to work with King Gateskin, Princess?"

"Yes, my sister and I would both be doing that."

Madrigal turned to speak with Izara and whispered in her ear before turning back to the group.

"We have discussed this and decided that we would give it a try and see how we like the new place and our duties."

"Oh, what duties would we have, Princesses?" Izara asked.

Navaeha replied, "Well, you would be mainly protecting the lands of Noella Province from any dangers. You would not be allowed beyond the borders of Sovorotskina where you will live."

King Gateskin added, "Also, you would not be allowed to eat any of the other animals on my land such as a horse, cow, chickens, pig, or wolves."

"Wolves? You have wolves?" Madrigal asked with wide and shocked eyes.

"Yes, but they are our pets and also keep our lands safe from other animals that could harm my people," the King answered.

"What would be our diet, King?" Izara enquired.

"More of those furry creatures I offered you today along with other food that my Queen would make for you. She is quite talented with creating new foods for our animals on our lands. In fact, the wolves have grown quite large due to her creations."

"I see," Madrigal stated with a creased brow.

"Does that seem fair to you both?" King Gateskin asked.

"Well, I guess it would work for us. We do agree that those creatures you offered us were the tastiest we have ever had," Madrigal added with a grin.

"Good, I am happy to hear that, dragons. It will be quite a journey for us and we must begin to return to my home. If you are ready."

Aharona and Navaeha jumped onto their dragons and told the two new dragons, "Please follow us to your new home."

"Wait a minute," Izara stressed.

"What is wrong?" Aharona turned to look at the dragon.

"What if we don't like our new home? Can we return here?"

"Of course you can," Aharona replied with a nod from King Gateskin.

"Okay, we are ready to go with you," the two dragons stated in unison.

CHAPTER FIFTEEN

King Gateskin contacted his wife through his thoughts that they were on their way home so she could prepare everything for them.

The children were excited to meet these new dragons and the idea of having them live there with them. They had prepared an area for the dragons away from the barn and all the animals and wolves. They didn't want to see any problems arise if the dragons got too close to the other animals. King Gateskin had told them they could build this lair even though he wasn't sure whether he would be obtaining dragons or not. He knew the building could also be used for the visiting dragons when the dragon ladies returned.

Serena was in charge of making sure that the dragons had a shelter and a soft place to sleep. They put out large basins for water and others for the food that their mother was preparing now. The children had built a large lair of sorts with the help of many of the guards and a little magic thrown in. It was quite an impressive building being well over 75 feet high so that the dragons wouldn't feel claustrophobic.

It had wide double doors that could open out and stay that way or close at a press of a lever. The dragons would be taught how to open and close them.

The children stood back to admire their work and slapped hands with one another in congratulations.

"I think Father will be pleased with this structure. Don't you both think so?" Serena asked.

"You bet he will," Simon announced with a grin.

"Yes, of course! He will love it," Catalina added with a laugh.

"We should go see if Mother needs any help with the food preparation," Serena stated as she led the way to their mother's workshop.

Inside the shop they saw their mother and Uncle Hotenfaran working over a large table that was covered with all kinds of items that they mixed and matched together forming one large ball. They spread their hands over the ball and recited spells to form it together.

The children were fascinated and didn't move any closer but waited for their mother to notice them.

"I know you are here, children," Queen Solinara announced in a soft voice.

"Oh, sorry, Mother. We didn't want to disturb you. You both were deep in concentration with the spells," Serena said.

"We are almost finished. We have a large amount already completed. This is the last of it. We will put it all into four huge tubs for the dragons when they get here. I'm sure they will be hungry. We will have four dragons here since Aharona and Navaeha are escorting the new dragons. The ladies will be staying for a while until they can train the dragons to obey your father's commands."

"How long will they be here, Mother?" Simon asked, clearly curious.

"They will be here with us for two weeks; your father told me. If they don't work out, the sisters and the four dragons will return to Dragonaria."

"But what if they love it here, Mother?" Catalina asked, with her fingers crossed.

"We will see, dear. Don't get your hopes up. These dragons are wild creatures and don't usually like change, especially if the change is to be permanent."

"Oh, I think they are going to love it here and us too!" Catalina added, enthusiastically.

"I hope they do, sweetheart. I surely hope they do," their mother replied.

"Do you need our help lifting the tubs, Mother. They look awfully heavy," Serena inquired.

"Yes, I think if we all add a little magic to them, they will be easier to carry."

Uncle Hotenfaran lifted the back end of the first tub and Queen Solinara lifted the front while the three children lifted the sides. It was much easier to move quickly out of the workshop and over to the dragons' new home a little distance away. They made three more trips and all was soon settled in the dragons' lair.

Catalina whooped with joy when her mother spread a spell over her to enable her to fly and still wore a wide smile as they landed. She was not able to fly on her own.

"Come with me, children. I need some help getting the quarters ready for the ladies and some food prepared for everyone."

Serena hurried ahead to help with the food preparation while her siblings were instructed to go to the addition of their home to get the beds and areas clean. This addition was once used for other visitors from Votovia. King Gateskin created this addition that could be stretched even larger if needed. He could also shrink it when it wasn't in use which is how it was now. They had to use a spell that their father had created to increase the size to fit the visitors a little more comfortably.

There would be two bedrooms, a kitchen, living area and a bathing room. They dusted and swept the areas and put clean towels in the bath and sheets, blankets and pillows on the beds. There was also plenty of storage space for the ladies to put their belongings.

After stepping back to look over their work, they smiled and went back to see if their mother and sister needed more help.

Serena and Solinara were humming a tune and working in tandem preparing sandwiches, drinks and pastries. Magic was flying back and forth through some powerful spells.

Simon and Catalina watched in awe as the sandwiches appeared from thin air and settled onto platters on the table along with drinks and all kinds of pastries and cookies.

Simon spoke up, "Can we have a cookie, Mother?"

"I think you should wait for our company to get here. I'm sure there are plenty but it would be nice to be outside to greet them. Your father said they are almost here. Get cleaned up and go outside now."

Simon and Catalina rushed to the bathing room and hurried back out to be first to greet the guests.

There was a wind that grew in intensity as they looked up to see black shapes coming their way. Queen Solinara concentrated and the shapes were defined into four dragons, and King Gateskin, Spindle, and the guards in the rear.

"Wow, look at them, Mother!" Serena exclaimed. "They are beautiful!"

"Yeah! They really are and they are going to be our very own dragons!" Simon and Catalina exclaimed.

"Come with me, children. Stand back a way. They will cause a gust of wind that could whip you up and cast you aside," their mother instructed.

CHAPTER SIXTEEN

In Parotovina children looked up when they felt a disturbance in the air. What they saw frightened them, causing them to run home and tell their parents what they saw.

One guard didn't flee but kept looking up and focusing on the shapes. He went to the castle to inform the King and Queen of Parotovina what he witnessed. He was sure he would be rewarded for doing so.

In the other lands of Merlina, Amora, Merona and Votovia people ran for cover when they saw many black shapes flying overhead.

King Cavelan of Votovia saw the shapes from his castle window and hurried to his drawing room to contact King Gateskin for it appeared that the shapes were headed toward Sovorotskina.

Votovia was the closest to the land of Sovorotskina where his close friend, King Gateskin lived. He and Gateskin had worked together to find and return the descendants of the Taken Ones. They always shared their concerns over the dangers that Parotovina brought to the other lands. Cavelan feared that maybe this was another thing that King Kaposkaran was sending their way to wreak havoc on their lands.

Back on Sovorotskina King Gateskin led the group to an open area to land far enough away from his home and his family who he could see standing in the distance to greet them.

Once everyone was settled down on the ground the ladies jumped off their dragons and spoke to them. "It will be up to you two to watch over Madrigal and Izara to make sure they stay out of trouble and don't eat anything they are not supposed to eat."

"We will do our best, Mistresses," Callum announced as he exchanged wary glances at the new dragons and nodded to Evander.

King Gateskin went over to his family with Spindle and his guards following. Aharona and Navaeha stayed back with the dragons until they were told where to put the creatures.

"It's good to have you back home, Gateskin," Queen Solinara kissed her husband and gave him a firm hug which he avidly returned.

"It is always good to be home, my dear."

He turned to his three children and hugged them all and whispered, "We have two dragons!"

The children jumped up and down and cheered, causing the dragons to flutter their wings and settle down again as they waited to meet their new family and home.

"Can we meet them now, Father?" Serena asked as she eyed the two dragons who were looking back at her and her siblings. Being the oldest of the three she tried not to sound too eager and put on her grown-up face. After all, she was a teenager and nearly an adult.

"We must get everyone settled first, Serena. Is the dragons' lair ready for them?"

"Oh, yes, Father. I can't wait for you to see it. I think we did an outstanding job."

"Good. Let's go see it now before we bring the dragons there."

Serena hurried forward to lead the way with her father close behind. He told his wife what he was going to do first so she could instruct the visitors to wait until he came back.

The lair was so large that it soon came into focus from where they stood.

"Well, you have done a wonderful job, Serena. I am proud of you."

"Thank you, Father. Of course, I had help from my siblings and the guards with a little magic thrown in."

Spindle beamed at Serena and nodded his approval causing her to blush crimson.

"Hmm, I see," Gateskin said, noticing the color blooming on his daughter's cheeks. "Well, it is superb. I'm sure the dragons will be quite comfortable here. They may like it so much that they will want to stay."

"Do you think they will, Father? I thought they were only on loan for two weeks. That's what Mother told me."

"Well, that is the plan. They need to be trained first over the two weeks. Afterwards we will see if they are receptive to my commands after instructions by Aharona and Navaeha. These two women are adept at this training since they have trained their own dragons as well as others."

"Well, Aharona and Navaeha did a good job with their own dragons. I love Callum and Evander. They are so different but both obey their mistresses. Does that mean that you will be the new dragons' master?"

"Yes, I expect that will be the case, Serena. They will be trained to listen to my commands eventually. We need to be patient with them. They have not had masters and have been on their own."

"Can we meet them now, Father?"

"Of course you can. Let's bring them to their new home."

Serena rushed back to tell her mother and siblings that they were ready to escort the dragons to their lair.

Simon and Catalina waited until their father gave them the sign that they could come closer to the dragons in order to meet them.

King Gateskin walked over to the dragon ladies and told them to follow him with all four dragons.

Aharona and Navaeha nodded and instructed the four dragons to follow them.

Callum and Evander turned to the two new dragons, Madrigal and Izara, and told them they were to follow close behind and not cause a wind around them. The two new dragons were in awe of Callum and Evander and would do anything they asked of them.

Madrigal and Izara nodded and followed, keeping their wings tucked close to their bodies. They surveyed the area around them as they walked along. Their noses and ears picking up many intriguing scents and sounds.

CHAPTER SEVENTEEN

The four dragons arrived at the lair and stopped as instructed by Aharona and Navaeha. They settled down to meet their new master's family.

Serena led her brother and sister over to meet Madrigal and Izara. "It is a pleasure to meet you both," Serena said as she waved at the dragons and stepped aside for her siblings to do the same.

"It is an honor to meet you all too," Madrigal stated after being nudged by Callum to return the children's greetings.

"Yes, it is an honor, I agree," stated Izara as she tried to meet the eyes of the children who kept staring at her. She was a little out of her element on this new land and did not feel comfortable yet. She found her mind wandering as her nose twitched with the new scents that caused her stomach to growl.

King Gateskin stepped closer to the two dragons and told them, "Follow me to your new lair. It was created by my eldest daughter, Serena, her siblings, and several of my guards."

Madrigal moved into the lair and looked up. He felt at once at peace with all the space around him. He sighed in relief that he and Izara would not be in cages as he had expected.

He whispered to Izara, "Look at this magnificent place. It is so spacious. There are even large shelves for us to sleep on."

"Yes, I think it's perfect for us. Do you think we will stay longer than the time they said we would be here?"

"We will see, Izara. There are many things we have to learn about this land and our new master and his family. Also, I am curious about all the enticing smells here."

"Hmm, I agree, Madrigal. I would love to taste some of them. Wouldn't you?"

"We need to find out what we can eat before we taste anything, Izara."

"Okay. I will rein in my hunger. But I hope they plan on feeding us soon. The long trip has made me hungrier than I ever thought possible."

Before Madrigal could respond to his mate, King Gateskin spoke. "I would imagine that you are hungry and thirsty. We have special food created by my talented wife for you to enjoy and afterward you can take a much-needed rest."

"That does sound good to our ears, King Gateskin," Madrigal piped up.

While the dragons were conversing with King Gateskin, Queen Solinara and their children came into the lair and uncovered the bowls that they had brought in earlier with the food and water.

Once the two dragons smelled the enticing aroma coming from the bowls, they quickly went to inspect them. Looking up at the King, they waited for him to say it was okay to eat.

King Gateskin nodded and they gulped down as much as they could in between breaths and burps causing the group to laugh at their atrocious eating behavior.

Callum and Evander were given permission from their mistresses to join in the eating from their own bowls which they did as daintily as they could to set an example for the other two dragons.

Aharona and Navaeha shook their heads in disbelief but laughed along with everyone else before saying, "Don't worry we will take care of this soon, King Gateskin. We promise that they won't be so clumsy about eating. Though I was surprised to see that they looked to you for directions when to eat even without our prompting."

King Gateskin said, "Yes, I saw that, Aarona. Maybe It won't be as difficult as we expected. Their behavior is okay for now. I expect they are hungry and tired from the long journey as we all are. Let's go to my house. My wife has prepared something for all of us too."

As Gateskin announced this, Solinara was already on her way home with the children behind her chattering away about the dragons.

Everyone followed the Queen and her children excluding the several guards who were on the outside and guarding the area. Spindle waved at them that it was time for them to get something to eat too.

Once everyone was settled and had quenched their thirst and filled their bellies, King Gateskin brought the dragon ladies into the extension of his home so that they could rest up until their first lessons began in the morning for the dragons. They all needed to rest and recharge for the first day of instructions. Aharona and Navaeha knew it wasn't going to be easy since these two dragons were not trained in any way and always did whatever they had wanted to do on their own.

King Gateskin thanked Spindle and the rest of the guards as they left to go on alert as he had instructed.

Gateskin went into his conference room when he heard a beeping sound coming from his Conference Call window. Someone was trying to contact him.

He opened up the Channel Spell to see the troubled look on the face of his good friend, King Cavelan from Votovia.

CHAPTER EIGHTEEN

"Oh, Gateskin! I am relieved to see you are all right. My people and I saw the black shapes flying into Sovorotskina. Are you or your people in danger?"

"No, we are all fine, Cavelan. I was planning to contact you and the other rulers of the villages as soon as we were all settled here."

"You have visitors? Those shapes we saw were expected by you?"

"Yes, I was one of those shapes along with Spindle, my head guard, and several other guards who traveled with us."

"Hmm, I see. You will be explaining more, I expect," Cavelan expressed his curiosity and concern.

"Of course, my friend. Do you remember when the dragons visited us here from Dragonaria?"

"Yes, they were quite magnificent."

"Well, we now have two of our own who will be trained by the dragon ladies who came with us."

"Two dragons? Of your own?"

"Yes, isn't that wonderful?"

"Well, I guess but I don't understand why," Cavelan stated with a confused expression.

"I will explain, I promise. We have had, as you know, many problems with Parotovina and King Kaposkaran and Queen Beregina. I wanted to ensure that we would always be safe here. That is why I wanted a trial with two dragons who would be trained by Aharona and Navaeha from Dragonaria. They assured me that this would be possible."

"They are going to train the dragons to take your commands and stay in Noella Province?"

"That's what is planned. This is on a trial basis for two weeks. If they don't work out, they will return to their home on Dragonaria."

"This is all so unbelievable, Gateskin. When you relate all this to the other rulers, what do you think they will say? Will they be averse to this?"

"Are you averse to this, Cavelan?" Gateskin scrutinized his friend's expression.

"Well, not exactly. I am just surprised. I knew you enjoyed having the dragons here before to assist you in finding the chest that houses the Medallion."

"We think the chest houses the Medallion, Cavelan. I have yet to open it. My wizards are keeping it in their care and examining it thoroughly for safety before we open it. Also, we found a silver mine buried inside the mountain next to the chest. I gave the silver to the blacksmith to use to make plates and whatever else he chose to create."

"That is a wise thing to do, my friend, about keeping the chest protected by the Wizards. Who knows what is in there. As for the silver, that is interesting that your blacksmith will create items from it. I would love to see them sometime."

"Of course, I will have the blacksmith bring some by so I can show you. I am interested in seeing them myself."

"Thank you, Gateskin. I look forward to that."

"These dragons may be beneficial in assisting me with the chest too. I have many plans for them to help make our lands stronger and resilient to any Dark Magic forces and from any other issues with Kaposkaran."

"I agree that we can use all the help to keep him at bay. He is dangerous as well as his wife and those under his rule."

"How are the new dragons adjusting to the land and climate difference, Gateskin?"

"Too soon to tell. They are settled in their new lair that my three children and my guards built for them. They appear to be quite happy there and also with the food Solinara and Hotenfaran created for them."

"I can believe that, Gateskin. Solinara and Hotenfaran are quite talented and creative in magical ways and can create something out of thin air."

"Yes, they can, Cavelan. They certainly can."

"Are you going to tell the other rulers soon about these dragons? What about Kaposkaran?"

"I plan to tell them all now. If you stay on the line, I will add them into the Conference Call to explain what I just did with you. If you feel like adding something after I finish, please feel free to do so."

"It would be my honor to support you, my friend. If you need anything at all, I am here for you."

"I know you are, Cavelan. You are always there for me as I am for you. I appreciate your support. Well, let's get this over with, shall we?"

Cavelan nodded as the calls were sent to the other villages in the south of Noella Province – Amora, Parotovina, Merlina and the central village of Merona last of all.

Gateskin waited for the windows in the rulers' conference rooms to open. After a few minutes, King Noderan of Amora popped in, next came The Healers of Merona, King Zuri of Merlina and last of all, King Kaposkaran of Parotovina who was looking his usual disgruntled self for being disturbed.

"Welcome, gentleman, to this Conference Call. I have some important news to share with you all."

King Kaposkaran spoke up, "I feel that you need to explain yourself, Gateskin. My people have been sharing with me something disturbing, to say the least."

"Have they?" Gateskin answered. He expected nothing less from this man. Kaposkaran's remarks were already causing disruption in his Conference Call.

"Well, are you going to explain yourself?" Kaposkaran asked, with a deep frown and grunt of disapproval.

"I will if you stop interrupting me so rudely, Kaposkaran," Gateskin tempered back.

"We are all interested to hear this news, Kaposkaran. Please desist with your rudeness.

We have questions for Gateskin as you do," King Noderan of Amora stated.

"Thank you, Noderan. I appreciate your support." Gateskin began to explain what he previously had to Cavelan about the dragons being trained on Sovorotskina by the two ladies from Dragonaria. He waited for some feedback negative or positive from the rulers. What he received first was the shocked expressions on their faces and opened mouths with no words coming out.

"Well, where are all your questions and/or concerns, gentlemen?"

Kaposkaran began first, "I figured that you would do something like this! Are you trying to intimidate us with these dragons? Will you be killing me and my people?"

"Of course not, Kaposkaran. I have no plans to endanger any of you or your people. My purpose is to keep the dragons on my land only and away from the people. They will be well trained to obey my commands and those of my family in order to keep them here and away from your lands."

King Zuri of Merlina asked, "Will they be kept away from the animals that graze nearby?"

"Most definitely, Zuri. They will be well fed and taught to only eat what we give them."

"Hmm, I see. What if they venture out beyond your borders and into our lands? Will our people be safe?" King Noderan asked.

"Yes, I will assure you now that they will never leave this land unless I am with them," Gateskin reassured them.

"You haven't really explained what the dragons will be doing here," The Healers of Merona questioned.

"Well, I have many ways for them to assist me on my land. The other two dragons from Dragonaria have already lent a hand in finding the chest with the lost Medallion."

"Ahh, yes. Whatever happened to that? Did you open the chest, Gateskin?" Zuri asked.

"Not yet. My wizards are working on it now."

"Will you share what you find inside with us, Gateskin?" The Healers enquired.

"Yes, I plan to do that soon enough after the dragons are trained. It may take a couple of weeks to do this training."

"I think it is a fascinating prospect to have dragons on Noella Province, rulers. Don't you?" Cavelan asked with a smile on his face as he looked at all the discontented expressions on his fellow rulers' faces.

Gateskin winked at Cavelan and said, "Well, if you don't have any other questions or concerns, I will sign off and get back to you in two weeks after the training is completed. Good day, gentlemen."

Gateskin closed the windows on all the rulers except one, Cavelan's, who waited to speak with his friend some more.

"Can I call you back, Cavelan. I need to speak with Spindle. I'll be right back to you as soon as I can."

Cavelan said, "No problem, Gateskin. I will be here when you call back."

The King sent a message to Spindle about having the blacksmith bring over the items he made using the silver from the mine.

Spindle replied, "I will go see him shortly, King. I bet he must have several items completed by now."

***

The blacksmith was closing up his shop the time Spindle stopped by. He looked up at the Sprite and asked, "What brings you this way, Spindle? Do you need for me to make something for you?"

"Oh no, Alaric. The King sent me by to ask you about the silver and what you have made from it."

"Oh, yes. I was planning on bringing over the items I made as a gift to him. I put them into a sack over there."

Spindle flew over to where the blacksmith had pointed. There was a large sack under a shelf that looked to hold quite a few things. He was excited to see what they were.

"Come closer, Spindle. Maybe there is something you would like to bring to your parents. I did make a few items which are small enough for your mother to use to cook."

"Really? My mother would be thrilled to have something new for her cooking. She is always complaining about everything getting dented."

"Well, this is quite sturdy and thick enough to withstand most any use."

"Wow! These are incredible, Alaric! You did a wonderful job!"

"Thank you, Spindle. You are most kind. Oh, and this item is for you."

The blacksmith held out a tiny sword with sparkling stones on the hilt.

"You made this for me? I love it! Thank you!"

"I'm happy you like it, Spindle. I wanted to show my appreciation for all that you do to keep us safe," Alaric announced with a wide smile.

"These other items are for the Queen to use."

There were several bowls, dishes, cups and pans that would surely please the Queen plus a few knives and a sword that would be for the King.

"You can take them all with you if you can carry them, Spindle, or I can bring them by tomorrow."

"I think I can manage to carry them with a little bit of magic thrown in."

"Nicely done, Spindle," Alaric said enthusiastically as the Sprite hefted the load and flew away.

CHAPTER NINETEEN

Spindle arrived back at the King's house to present the silver pieces to him and his wife much to their surprise.

"These are beautiful!" Queen Solinara announced as she touched each item and marveled at the smooth texture and quality of the item made.

The King beamed when he saw the knives and sword. "These are incredible. I will stop by to thank Alaric in person tomorrow."

"Yes, I will join you. He was so kind to do all this for us," Solinara added.

"Did you notice something new?" Spindle spun around to show off his own sword that was now attached to his belt.

"That is quite a handsome sword, Spindle," Gateskin stated with a grin. "Did Alaric make that for you?"

"He most certainly did, King! He said he wanted to thank me for all that I do to keep the villagers safe."

"He is quite a talented blacksmith and a kind and thoughtful man."

"Yes, he is. He even made some items for my mother. I will bring them to her now."

"Amazing! They are so tiny! Just the right size for her," Solinara chuckled in delight.

"Well, enjoy your gifts, King and Queen. I can't wait to see my mother's face when I present these to her!"

"Goodnight, Spindle. Thanks for bringing these by," King Gateskin responded.

Anabal, Spindle's mother, cried when she saw the pans and plates that Alaric had created for her. She would be the envy of all the Sprites now, she thought. She would stop by tomorrow to thank the blacksmith in person with a cake.

***

Things were brewing in Parotovina. King Kaposkaran called his guards to a meeting in his conference room after hearing what King Gateskin had acquired. He had plans to somehow curtail King Gateskin's latest project.

The men whispered back and forth to each other as they waited for the King to explain this urgent meeting with them. They knew that something was going on in Sovorotskina after hearing the whispers amongst the villagers who spoke of some black shapes that were seen traveling overhead.

King Kaposkaran raised his hands and called out for quiet from his guards who snapped to attention at his voice.

"By this time, you have heard the rumors about the black shapes that flew over Noella Province. These shapes were dragons led by citizens of Dragonaria along with King Gateskin and his guards."

The guards mumbled amongst themselves at this news and hands were raised with questions that the King ignored.

He continued to explain, "These dragons will be residing in the village of Sovorotskina. King Gateskin's plans are to train them to listen to his commands. You all know what that will mean to our lands. He will have complete control over all of us. Our lives are in his hands now. I will not stand for that! I will fight back."

Voices were raised in alarm but the King raised his hands to quiet them down. "I am not finished, men!"

The voices silenced as they waited for more news.

"I will be sending several of you to visit Sovorotskina to spy on this training and do all you can to disrupt King Gateskin's plans. Do you understand what I mean, men?"

Many called out 'yes' in consent.

"I want six men who are willing to do this. Raise your hand or step forward if you agree."

More than a dozen men raised their hands to volunteer. They stepped forward as the King walked along and chose six of them to stay behind after dismissing the rest of his guards.

The six men stood at attention waiting to hear what their king wanted them to do and when their mission would begin.

"You have chosen to take on this mission. I expect that you know if you are not successful that you will lose your life along with your families. Do you understand the seriousness of this mission?"

The six men accepted individually as the King came up to each one. He instructed, "Go home to your families and tell them nothing of this mission but that you will be leaving for an indeterminate time frame. They are to be quiet about your leaving and not discuss this with anyone else. Do you understand?"

"Yes, King Kaposkaran," the men answered in unison.

"Good. Now you go home and prepare for this mission. You will not wear your uniforms but instead you must blend in with the other villagers of Sovorotskina. Wear appropriate clothes and do not stay together once you arrive at Sovorotskina. You will move throughout the land there and do what you can to wreak havoc all through the village while King Gateskin is training the dragons. Do you understand?"

"Yes," the men answered once again together.

King Kaposkaran waved his hands at the men dismissing them. He waited until they had left his conference room before summoning his wife, Queen Beregina.

"What is it, Kapo?" Queen Beregina asked, clearly displeased for being disturbed.

"Nice to see you, dear. I have news that might interest you. Maybe you can conjure up some of that Dark Magic again to assist in my plan."

"What? I thought you didn't want me to ever do that again after the last time with the growing moss."

The growing moss was created using Dark Magic by the Queen that was supposed to put all the Catlings to sleep who had invaded the land. It not only put these creatures to sleep but also any other animals that ate it. It had become a nuisance when it began to increase and move throughout the land. The moss had to be destroyed by fire after they had moved all the sleeping Catlings back to the UT, Unknown Territory.

"I know, but I changed my mind, dear. Listen to me. Once you hear what I have to say, you will understand how important it is that you do something to help."

After explaining what he had in mind, Beregina grinned and nodded eagerly that she was on board.

"Hmm, I thought you would change your mind eventually, Kapo. I knew you would need me to do this again. Well, I better get to work. It does take some effort to conjure it up again."

"Thank you, Ber."

"What did you call me?"

"Well, as long as you keep calling me Kapo, I am going to call you Ber!"

"Hmph, all right, Kaposkaran. We are even now."

"You bet we are, dear," Kaposkaran guffawed.

CHAPTER TWENTY

The King and Queen flew over to see the blacksmith to thank him in person for his kind gifts.

"Nice to see you both," Alaric said with a deep bow of respect.

"I brought you a casserole and some of my meat pies and gingersnaps. I'm sure your children will enjoy them."

"Thank you so much. You didn't have to do that, Queen, but I am grateful as will my wife be when she sees dinner all prepared for tonight," Alaric laughed heartily.

"Thank you again, Alaric. If you need more silver, please let me know. There is plenty more where that came from in the mine."

"I do have some left, King. But thank you. I definitely will tell you when I run out."

"We must be on our way, Alaric. But we appreciate your efforts and see that you are quite talented. Give your wife and children our love."

"Thank you. I will, King and Queen. It was a pleasure to see you both." Alaric bowed again.

***

Gateskin called King Cavelan back to discuss more after the Conference Call was ended with the other rulers.

"Sorry I'm just getting back to you. I had to visit with our blacksmith. He was kind enough to gift us some of the items he created using the silver from the mine we found. Well, what do you think about all this with the dragons, Cavelan?"

"That is interesting. I must see these silver items when I visit another time. As for the dragons, I am excited for you, my friend. I would love to be there to see them and how this works. I may want one or two dragons of my own."

"I figured you might, Cavelan. I don't know if King Marcellus would be agreeable to sending more dragons here though. I had a difficult time convincing him to allow us to take two. In fact,

I have Queen Isla to thank for finally turning things around for me. She somehow convinced her husband that it would be a good thing to do."

"I see. The woman was the one who won him over? That would work with me too. My wife always wins the arguments."

"Yes, I agree. They are stronger than we are, but don't tell them that, Cavelan," Gateskin snickered.

"You don't have to worry about that. I don't want any trouble on the home front."

"You are always welcome to come visit, Cavelan. I plan to begin the training tomorrow early. My trainers, the Dragonarians, are resting now as well as the dragons. It was a long and tiring journey from their island to Noella Province. I think everyone needs to take a breather for a little while."

"I can imagine it was. I would enjoy coming to visit you. I will tell Queen Savina that it is strictly business and that I cannot bring her. She may give me a hard time about not visiting with your wife. They have become good friends as we have."

"Well, I don't think it would be a problem if you brought her with you. Solinara would be happy to have her visit. They would keep each other busy and away from the dragons. Solinara knows there is an element of danger while the dragons are being trained. She plans to keep the children away from here too."

"Okay, I will tell her this. She can come as long as she stays clear of all this with your wife."

"Good. I will relay this to Solinara. That way she will be preoccupied and stop asking me about the dragons' every move."

"I only hope that I don't get the same thing from my wife once she knows that you have four dragons here now and will keep two to stay on. I know she will want a couple of her own."

Gateskin laughed out loud at this and said, "Don't worry. These dragons can be scary and just looking at them may change her mind quickly."

"I can only hope so, Gateskin. Well, I'll let you go. You must be tired from your long journey too. See you tomorrow bright and early."

"Good night, Cavelan."

Gateskin closed the Conference Call and went to see his wife to tell her to expect a couple of visitors tomorrow.

***

Spindle was coming to see the King before he finished his rounds and retired for the night. He knocked on the King's door and waited.

"Spindle, come in. You must be tired. Is everything in order?" Gateskin asked and he noticed that the Sprite still had his sword in his scabbard on his belt.

"Oh, yes, King. I just wanted to tell you how well everything went today with the dragons. They appeared to be quite happy with their lair. I checked in on them on my way here and they were fast asleep. I also checked in the barn and the animals were also asleep. The wolves were roaming back and forth and I assured them that all is safe for them and their families. They were a little disturbed to see the new dragons coming here."

"I imagine they would be. I will speak with them myself before I retire. Thank you for all that you do for me, Spindle. I can't ask for a better Head Guard than you."

"My pleasure, King. I try my best and feel it is an honor to serve you and your people."

"Well, be on your way home. I'm sure your parents won't sleep until you are safely in the tree with them."

"You are right about that, King. They don't care how old I am, they still worry as if I were a child."

"All parents do that, Spindle. Age doesn't matter to us. See you bright and early tomorrow when we will begin the training."

"I look forward to that, King. I want to make sure those new dragons don't want to eat me. The other two are used to me now and know that I don't taste good. I just have to convince the new ones of the same thing. Good night, King."

"I'm sure you will find a way, Spindle," Gateskin chuckled.

After closing the door, Gateskin went to finish explaining to his wife what was going to take place in the morning.

"Who was that, Gateskin?" Solinara asked.

"Spindle came to say good night and relate what he did on his rounds. All is well, dear. No worries."

"That's nice to hear. Now what were you going to tell me, Gateskin?"

Gateskin explained about his plans for the morning and that they were going to have more visitors.

"Oh, how wonderful! I haven't visited with my good friend, Savina, in a long time. We have so much to share. We had better get to sleep now for tomorrow will bring much to do."

"I agree, Solinara. Are the children asleep yet?"

"I bet they are still awake talking together. They are all in Serena's room the last time I checked."

Gateskin peeked in his oldest daughter's room and sure enough all three were chattering away about the dragons."

"Hi Father! We were discussing which dragon we liked the best," Serena announced.

"Which one is that?" Gateskin inquired.

"Well, that is the problem, Father. We can't decide since we really don't know them well enough to choose. They are different like Callum and Evander are, not only in colors but also in temperaments."

"I agree with you, Simon. They are like people. We are all different too."

"Yes, that is right, Father," Catalina announced with a proud grin. "You are always right!"

"Well, maybe you better tell that to your mother. On second thought, please don't!" Gateskin laughed.

"Maybe Mother wouldn't like that, right?" Catalina asked, with a puzzled look.

"That is correct, sweetheart. Let's forget I ever mentioned that. Okay?"

"Okay, Father. I guess," she responded as she shrugged her shoulders.

"Tomorrow will be a busy day for everyone. You three will be responsible to keep watch over the animals in the barn, the wolves and picking the vegetables from the garden for your mother. We are expecting more company from Votovia, King Cavelan and Queen Savina."

"Really? Are the kids coming too?"

"No, I don't think so. You will be too busy to entertain them anyway."

"I guess so," Simon said, in disappointment.

"Goodnight children, sleep well."

"Goodnight, Father," they responded as they went to their respective bedrooms.

The coming days would bring more trouble than they could ever imagine.

CHAPTER TWENTY-ONE

Queen Solinara was the first to rise this busy morning. She began to prepare breakfast for her family with her head spinning about all that was going to take place this day with the dragons.

King Gateskin soon joined her in the kitchen to lend a hand. Their three children were already up feeding the animals in the barn and the wolves who were pacing back and forth as they waited to be fed.

The dragons heard the barn animals moving about and pushed open the doors to their lair as they looked out to see what was happening in this new land.

Catalina called out to the dragons who flew above her. "We are bringing your food to you. Wait in your lair."

The dragons returned to their lair when they heard food and settled down to wait for this delicious food that they had already tasted the night before. Their large jaws began to drool in anticipation, pooling at their feet.

Serena asked Simon, "You need to help me bring in the dragons' food. The tubs are extremely heavy."

"Don't worry. I can fly them over to the lair but you need to help me lift them up first with a little magic."

"I was planning to do that but flying them over with magic might be quicker. Let's do it!"

Catalina clapped her hands as she watched her siblings flying over to the dragons' lair with the large tubs between them. "Wow! That is perfect!" she exclaimed as her father came up behind her.

"Oh, I didn't know my children could be so clever to think of delivering the dragons' food this way. Great idea!" Gateskin announced.

"I didn't hear you coming, Father. You made me jump!" Catalina exclaimed.

"Sorry, sweetheart. Have you seen the dragons come out of their lair yet?"

"Yes, I did. I told them to go back and wait for their food."

"You did? Did they listen?"

"Of course, they did. They are our dragons now and have to obey if they want food."

"Right, I didn't think of it that way," he chuckled as he hugged his youngest daughter. She was always the outspoken one and caused him much joy each time she spoke up about something. She was fearless and adorable with her golden curls and bright blue eyes. She was growing up so fast, almost twelve and her face had lost its baby fat years ago.

Gateskin sighed and watched his children, no longer babies with such surprising skills and powers that kept increasing. Serena was already sixteen with long golden hair and blue eyes. Simon was fourteen, light brown hair and green eyes, always trying to be the man in every situation. Gateskin couldn't help trying to keep them young in his mind and heart to protect them.

Inside the lair, Serena and Simon set down the tubs full of food that their mother and uncle had made ahead of time, and stepped back so that the dragons could sniff and eat their fill.

The two children waited before leaving the lair when Madrigal spoke up, "Thank you for this delicious food. We have never had anything like it before and now don't want anything else."

"You are quite welcome, Madrigal. Our mother and uncle created this for you. They will be pleased to hear that you are enjoying it and their efforts," Serena responded with a curtsy.

"Please do not bow to us, Princess. It should be us bowing to you. Right, Izara?"

Izara grunted and continued to eat, ignoring her mate's words.

"I guess Izara doesn't like the food as much as you do, Madrigal," Simon stated with a frown.

"Oh, she will not admit that it is good but try to take it away from her. Please, do not. I am only saying that facetiously," the dragon warned.

"We weren't planning to get near her while she is eating," the children stated in a serious tone.

"Are you happy to be here, Madrigal?" Simon asked in a hesitant manner.

"It is a little early to say but I am feeling better about being here. You have been most kind to us."

"We are happy to have you and feel fortunate that you agreed to come and give us a chance to get to know you better," Serena said.

"We will need time to do that and learn how to interact with all of you. I'm sure Aharona and Navaeha have many things to teach us. We will try to cooperate. At least I will. I can't speak for Izara. She has her own mind."

"Are you happy to be here, Izara?" Serena inquired.

Izara licked the last vestiges out of her tub and burped loudly and as obnoxiously as she could, never meeting Serena's eyes.

"I guess we will give her some time to adjust," Simon added as he winked at Madrigal who grinned back at him.

King Gateskin came into the lair after the last exchange between his children and the dragons. "I see you enjoyed your food," he announced.

"Of course, King Gateskin. It was delicious as I remembered last night," Madrigal said as he bowed to the King.

"What about you, Izara? Are you satisfied with your meal?" Gateskin said as he waited for her reply.

Madrigal whispered to his mate, "You need to answer the King. He is to be our new master. It is not good to be rude when you have been treated so well."

"I will not answer until I see what they have for us to do here. After that, I will give my opinion about everything."

"Whatever you want to do, Izara. But don't wait too long. I like it here already. I wouldn't want you to go back to Dragonaria without me."

"What? You would do that? You would stay here without me, Madrigal?"

King Gateskin cleared his throat and said, "We will begin your training as soon as Aharona and Navaeha have had their breakfast. That will give you time to discuss this privately." Gateskin took his children aside and told them to follow him as quietly as they could out of the lair and back to the house for breakfast.

Shortly behind the King and his children, Evander and Callum snuck out of the lair. They did not want to be in the middle of the other dragons' argument. They flew over to a wooded area to take a quick nap after their full stomachs from breakfast.

King Gateskin noticed them and nodded his approval.

"Wow, Izara is not as nice as Madrigal, Father," Simon stated with a sigh.

"Each dragon reacts to change in their own way as we do. Don't you remember how excited you all were when we got wolves, but the wolves were not as receptive as you were. They, in time, got used to their new home. So will the dragons in due time."

"I guess you are right, Father," Simon responded.

"I think they will grow to love us and our land, Father," Serena said with a grin. "I know they will. Izara will come around soon too. I think she is just being stubborn and doesn't want to admit anything right now."

"You may be correct about that, Serena."

"Yes, I agree with Serena," Catalina spoke up. "Izara is just being stubborn like me sometimes."

"Yes, I can see that, sweetheart," Gateskin laughed.

Breakfast was in full swing when the children and Gateskin came into the kitchen. There were plenty of eggs, pancakes and sausages in the steaming new silver platters which kept filling up as each person took their share. Plates of toast were set next and did the same thing, filling up before they emptied completely.

"I like this abundancy, Aharona, don't you? I wish we could do this on our island."

"I wish I could teach you," Queen Solinara said with a giggle. "But I'm afraid that it can't be taught."

Voices could be heard outside as their visitors, King Cavelan and Queen Savina arrived and were welcomed in to eat.

"It's so wonderful to see you both. Please sit down and join us. There's plenty to eat for everyone," Queen Solinara announced.

"It's good to be here. Thank you. We did eat a little before we left home but I can always find room for some of your exceptional food, Solinara," King Cavelan said as he made himself at home as he reached for a few pancakes.

Queen Savina shook her head at her husband and took a seat and a cup of coffee as she spoke to Queen Solinara and thanked her for welcoming them.

"Are you sure you don't want anything to eat, Savina?"

"Maybe I will try some eggs. We don't have as many chickens at home as you do, Solinara. Maybe we need a little of your magic to get them to lay some eggs."

"I would be happy to help in that way, Savina," Solinara giggled in response.

"It's a pleasure to see you again, ladies," Queen Savina said to Aharona and Navaeha.

"It is our pleasure, Queen Savina," Aharona responded as she pushed herself away from the table. "We have a busy day ahead of us. If you will please excuse us, Queen Solinara and Queen Savina. We need to get to work."

"Of course. We look forward to hearing how your first day of training goes, ladies. Good luck," Solinara said.

Queen Savina sipped her coffee and admired the silver platters that held all the food.

"What lovely platters, Solinara!"

"Oh yes, these were created by our village blacksmith, Alaric, using the silver the dragons found from Mt. Ailylene. He is a talented artist, don't you think?"

"Yes, most definitely he is!" Savina gushed.

***

Back in the lair the two dragons were still arguing about their previous conversation. At least one was arguing while the other was listening.

CHAPTER TWENTY-TWO

King Gateskin and King Cavelan followed the dragon ladies shortly after they finished eating. They wanted to give the ladies some time to speak to the new dragons.

Gateskin turned to Cavelan as they walked toward the dragons' lair several minutes afterwards. "When I left the dragons, they were arguing about whether they liked it here or not. Well actually, it was the female dragon, Izara, who was arguing while her mate, Madrigal, was listening."

"Hmm, that does sound familiar, Gateskin," Cavelan laughed but turned serious as he said, "I hope they are not going to leave before they are trained."

"I don't think they will, my friend. Madrigal is a smart one and knows how far to push his mate. Izara appears to like to rile him up to see what he will do. I don't think she means any harm to anyone, or at least I hope not."

"Well, I guess we will find out soon enough, Gateskin. There they are with the ladies. They look peaceful at least."

"I guess so but look at Izara's face. She is the smaller one with purple scales and matching eyes while Madrigal is turquoise and has eyes very close to the color also of his scales. They are quite a striking pair."

"I agree. They are magnificent creatures. I can see Izara has a furrowed brow and her scales appear to be bristling. What are the ladies going to do first?" Cavelan enquired.

"We will see," Gateskin responded as he held his breath watching the ladies move the dragons around with a wave of their hands.

***

While the ladies and kings were preoccupied with the dragons' training, two creatures were creeping closer for a look at what was transpiring.

Spindle flew above the two creatures and called out to King Gateskin, "Look who is here, King."

Gateskin turned around and spied the two Quintaroons, in their human forms, watching the dragons.

"What are you two doing here? Who is watching over you? You are not supposed to be out and about by yourselves."

"We are sorry but we heard the commotion of the dragons coming and wanted to see them in action. Spindle is watching over us. We called him to let us out of our house," Quintal explained in a shaky voice.

"We apologize if we did anything wrong, King," Talon added as he bowed his head.

"Well, I don't see anything wrong as long as Spindle keeps an eye on you. Stay back. I don't want you to upset the dragons while they are training. They may sense that you are not human and react in a negative way."

"Oh, we don't want that to happen. They could hurt us or worse, kill us," Quintal exclaimed in alarm. "Maybe we better return to our home,

Talon. I don't want to think about what the dragons could do to us."

"Well, if we changed, we could fight them," Talon stressed.

"I wouldn't do that if I were you," Gateskin stated firmly with a deep frown as he directed Spindle to take the Quintaroons away immediately. "Make sure they do not come out again until after the dragons are done training, Spindle."

"Of course, King. I tried to keep them away from here. We were supposed to only go for a stroll since they were complaining of being restless."

"You can take them for a stroll elsewhere, okay?"

"Whatever you say, King. No problem whatsoever," Spindle said as he pushed the Quintaroons toward the direction of their home.

The Quintaroons whispered to each other during the walk back to their place. They were disappointed but tried not to show their displeasure to Spindle as he flew up to their house and opened the door for them. Spindle quickly locked the door from the outside and pocketed the key on his person.

He could hear the Quintaroons complaining loudly about being locked in and that no one trusted them to behave.

Spindle chuckled to himself as he flew back to the King's side to see if there was anything else he needed him to do.

Gateskin looked up when he felt the breeze pick up from Spindle's wings overhead. "Did they give you any trouble, Spindle?"

"Not really, King. They complained as usual but that is what they do. I think they will have to come to terms about things, especially about what Talon said to you."

"I think Talon likes to show bravado to Quintal."

"Right, I agree, King. He does act like he is braver than he really is. Though I don't like the idea that they want to change back to their Quintaroon states. That could be problematic, don't you think, King?"

"Yes, I do, Spindle. That is why you will keep a close watch over them and a tight rein, my little man. I know you are quite capable of doing that. Also, please keep watch over the skies and have your fellow Sprites do the same for anyone coming from the other lands. I know they want to see what is transpiring here also."

"I will do my best, King. I will contact my fellow Sprites right away and report back to you if they see anything coming this way."

"Thank you, Spindle. I couldn't ask for a better Head Guard than you."

"Thank you, Sir!" Spindle bowed as he flew up to the trees and prepared to contact his fellow Sprites right away.

Spindle looked over the tree line and watched the skies as he messaged the other Sprites. These little tree creatures were clever and magical in many ways. They had previously been instrumental in aiding King Gateskin and his children to traverse the deep woods to go to Parotovina and bring back the descendants of the Taken Ones. Without their assistance, the task would not have been successful.

The Sprites lived throughout the wooded areas of Noella Province and even throughout some of the Unknown Territory where other creatures who were dangerous lived. They stayed hidden in the trees but always alert to what was going on around them. They were valuable as sentries to all the lands but especially to Sovorotskina and King Gateskin who they revered.

Spindle and his family were indebted to the King for bringing back Spindle's long-lost uncle, Micah, who had been kidnapped along with the Taken Ones over a hundred years before. Sprites could live a long life of hundreds of years.

A signal was heard from the Sprites who would sing out in different sounds as warnings when danger was near. This is what Spindle now heard. He flew up above the trees and listened to what the other Sprites were transmitting to him.

CHAPTER TWENTY-THREE

The dragons were tiring as they were given a rest period before King Gateskin would join them for the first time as their new master.

Aharona beckoned King Gateskin closer so she could share what she wanted him to do. "Navaeha and I have been talking to the dragons and explaining what we are expecting of them. While they are resting for a few moments we wanted to explain to you what your role will be now that they know what they are supposed to do."

King Gateskin eagerly stepped forward and said, "I am ready to learn whatever there is to learn about handling these incredible creatures. I am in awe of them."

"Haha, don't let them know that. You are in command of them and not the other way around," Navaeha warned.

"I understand. Of course, I am ready for whatever you need me to do."

"Okay, step closer to the dragons and call out to them to come to you and sit," Aharona instructed.

Gateskin called out, "Madrigal and Izara, come here and sit."

The two dragons came out of their stupor that was putting them to sleep and looked toward the voice of the King. They slowly flew up and came closer and sat in front of King Gateskin and waited.

King Cavelan clapped in appreciation and called out, "Good job, Gateskin."

Gateskin smiled and waved at his friend and turned a serious face to the dragons who were sitting there looking at him expectantly.

He whispered to Aharona, "What do I do next?"

"Tell them to fly up above you, do a circle and come back down and sit again."

Gateskin did this and waited as he smiled in surprise that the dragons had listened to his commands so easily.

Izara was getting restless and began to move back and forth. She swayed as she clawed the earth around her feet.

Navaeha waved at her in warning to sit still and pay attention.

Aharona whispered to Gateskin, "Now tell them that you want to climb up on their backs one at a time while they sit still."

Gateskin looked in shock at her words, "You mean I will be flying on their backs already? What if they do not want me to do that? Do you think they are ready for this?"

"We won't know that until we try it, right?" Aharona stated with a wink.

"I suppose that is true. I will try Madrigal first then Izara."

"Good idea. If Izara sees you on Madrigal, she may be more receptive to having you sit on her back afterwards."

Gateskin whispered under his breath, "I certainly hope so." He looked back at Cavelan who was wide-eyed and shaking his head.

The King came closer to Madrigal and said in a firm voice, "Lay down, Madrigal, so I can get up on your back."

Madrigal did not hesitate to follow instructions and laid down so that Gateskin could hop up onto his scaly back.

Once the King was up on the dragon's back, he sat up taller and smiled as he patted the dragon on his head and felt the scales that were hard but cool and sharp to touch. He watched the sun shine over the scales creating a rainbow effect of purple and other colors. He found that he was holding his breath at the sight.

Madrigal turned his head to look at the King when he heard his intake of breath. "Are you all right, my king?"

"Oh, I'm fine, really fine in fact, Madrigal. I never knew this could be so moving being up on your magnificent back. You really are impressive creatures."

"I am honored to have you on my back, King. It is a pleasure to serve you. Don't tell Izara, but I am quite happy here and pleased to be your dragon at your service. I don't want to return to Dragonaria."

"Wow, I didn't expect that so early on, Madrigal. It is my honor also to have you here on my land. I hope that you will always feel this way."

"King Gateskin, try getting on Izara's back now," Aharona urged.

Gateskin easily hopped off Madrigal's back and went over to Izara who was lazing and closing her eyes.

"Izara, lay still so I can get on your back as I did with Madrigal."

"Why do you want to go on my back? Are we going back to my land?"

"No, I just want to climb up on your back."

"But why would you need to do that unless we are going somewhere?"

Aharona and Navaeha came up behind Gateskin to see what was holding him up from climbing onto Izara's back.

"What is the problem here, Izara?" Aharona raised her voice at the dragon and frowned.

"Who am I to listen to, you or this king?"

"Izara, that is rude to say. You know who you are supposed to obey," Navaeha scolded.

"Do I?" Izara turned and walked away and flew into the air back to the lair.

Madrigal came forward and sat in front of the King and said, "I apologize for my mate's rudeness. I don't know what came over her. She has been disgruntled since we arrived. I can't seem to get through to her that this is a good thing to do. We are so much better off here than on Dragonaria where we had to fend for ourselves. Here we are taken care of royally. We have this beautiful lair and delicious food. Who could ask for more?" Madrigal shook his head and looked at Gateskin with sadness in his eyes.

"I think she needs more time to adjust, Madrigal. Let's give her that for now. Tomorrow we will try again. Go to her and let her know that everything will be better tomorrow," Gateskin stated with a deep sigh.

The dragon headed back to the lair to discuss this more with his mate but turned back to the king before entering and shook his head in disbelief.

"It's okay, Madrigal. See you tomorrow," Gateskin stated and went to speak with the dragon ladies to discuss what they would do the next day.

"She will come around, King. I really believe Izara is happy here but doesn't want to admit it. I think she likes to give everyone a hard time no matter what," Aharona said.

"We really don't know her well enough to say otherwise, King," said Navaeha.

"We have two weeks to complete this training. We don't want her to get discouraged the first day. Let's give her some space," Gateskin responded.

"We will do whatever you say, King. Is there anything we can do for you with our own dragons while we are here?"

"Yes, I think there is. I have some building to do for the wolves. Can your dragons carry the fallen trees back here from the woods in the UT? I don't want my men to go there because of the creatures that are there. Do you remember the Catlings?"

"Oh, yes, I do," Navaeha shivered as she remembered her near miss with one of them on a previous visit.

King Cavelan was listening to what Navaeha said about the Catlings. He was curious and asked, "What can these cat-like creatures do?"

Gateskin spoke up, "The question is what can't they do, Cavelan. They are dangerous to all of us and all the other animals in the area. That's why we keep them at bay at all times with our barriers along the borders."

"Hmm, I see. I haven't seen any in Votovia or near the border there. Thank goodness for that."

"Maybe you should strengthen your borders to make sure they don't come your way, Cavelan. They did travel to Parotovina in the past. They found their way there somehow. They are resilient creatures and move around the UT but also are not afraid of venturing further outside of it if they can. There evidently was a breach in my southeastern border and roamed into Parotovina. I have since reinforced all the borders."

"I do remember there was a problem there. Yes, maybe I will increase the spells on my borders when we return home. In fact, I think we can leave now since I've seen the dragons and what you have done so far. You will keep me informed, won't you, Gateskin?"

"Of course, Cavelan. I will. I will see you back at my house as soon as I am through here."

"Okay. I will prepare my wife for departure. She always takes so long to say goodbye to your wife," Cavelan chuckled.

***

As the dragons flew up into the Unknown
Territory to fetch some of the trees that had
fallen, the Catlings prowled the borders and
watched the large dragons descend to their
home.

CHAPTER TWENTY-FOUR

Also, in the Unknown Territory, a being was flitting around and sitting up in the trees observing the dragons as they came to land nearby to gather the fallen trees.

This being was just a spark of light that had escaped from the chest that supposedly housed the lost Medallion. This spark had been watching everything going on not only in the Unknown Territory but also in all of Sovorotskina. It saw the four dragons and took in everything that they were doing. It had even ventured closer when no one was around to watch the dragons as they slept in their lair.

It could become invisible in that its light would dim or go out completely as it flitted around. The dragons never saw it. It was concerned about the Sprites, however, who were aware of everything.

***

Callum and Evander were busy carrying the tree limbs back and forth at the request of the King to an area outside the wolves' enclosure. The King, along with several guards, were preparing to build another larger hut for the growing population of wolves who roamed the borders and protected Sovorotskina from the Catlings who threatened to cross the borders in spite of the protective spells that King Gateskin had placed there.

The Sprites were flying back and forth as they watched the dragons complete their tasks. Spindle had warned them ahead of time that the dragons would be doing this.

One younger Sprite had spied something strange and had gone to find Spindle to tell him. Before he could get to Spindle, a strange thing happened, the Sprite suddenly burst into flame and disappeared.

The young Sprite's parents were looking for him later that day for supper. He never answered their chitters or calls to return home. The mother called out to the other neighboring Sprites to ask if they had seen her son. No one had.

The Sprite's father said, "I will go see Spindle. He will know what to do and how to find our son. Don't worry, dear. We will find him."

His wife sniffled and nodded.

Spindle was doing his usual rounds and checking on the Quintaroons once again when the Sprite called out to him from a nearby tree, "Spindle, I need to ask for your help."

"What's wrong?" Spindle turned away from the Quintaroon's door after warning them to behave until he could return later to take them out for a walk.

The Sprite told Spindle about his missing son. "I don't understand why he didn't answer. He always stays close by. He is still quite young and I do worry about him with the Catlings around. He knows that he needs to stay up high away from them in the highest branches. The Catlings do know how to climb but cannot get up that high for the branches are too thin."

"Don't worry, I will do my best to find him. Go stay with your wife. I will come see you as soon as I find him or at least to let you know what happened to him."

"Do you think something has happened to him, Spindle?"

"No, I didn't mean that. Go now. I will find him, I promise."

Spindle flew over to see the King and relayed this present situation. He was worried that maybe the Catlings had gotten the little Sprite or something else. He thought back to the day that he had spied some flashing light go by into the Unknown Territory. He hadn't thought too much about it at that time but now, it could be something.

King Gateskin was busy building the huts for the wolves when Spindle flew down to the King's shoulder.

"Ahh, Spindle. Did you come to assist us?"

"Well, I will if you need me. What I came for was to tell you something important. Maybe I should have mentioned it before but I didn't think it was anything to bother you with, my king."

"You have piqued my interest now, Spindle. Let me give instructions to the guards what to do next and we can move away from here and discuss this more."

Spindle nodded in assent and waited a short distance away from the other guards.

When King Gateskin came next to Spindle, the Sprite explained about the missing little Sprite and what he had seen before of a flashing light.

"Hmm, that is interesting. Are you going out to look for the Sprite? Do you think whatever this light is that it is responsible for the missing Sprite?"

"Maybe, I'm not sure. I don't even know what it is."

"Yes, I agree. If you need more men to help you search, I can send them along with you."

"No, this is in the Unknown Territory. It would not be safe for the men. I will enlist my fellow

Sprites to help me, King. I will let you know if and when I find him and if I see that light again."

"Good. I will wait to hear from you. Have you seen Mitteran lately?" Mitteran was the second Head Guard in command behind Spindle. He was previously from Parotovina and came here with his family to escape persecution from the evil king. He had promised to be loyal to King Gateskin and so far, he had been thoroughly devoted to King Gateskin.

"No. Do you want me to find him? Do you need him to do something?"

"Well, I could use his help here. If you find him, send him here. Okay?"

"Of course, King. Right away." Spindle flew high up into the trees and looked far and wide for any sign of the little Sprite and Mitteran.

CHAPTER TWENTY-FIVE

Mitteran was wandering around the borders and keeping an eye on the Catlings who were strolling back and forth much too close to the borders of Sovorotskina. He had been on patrol all morning without telling the King or Spindle.

He was concerned about the restlessness of the Catlings. Something was bothering them. They didn't appear to be afraid of anything but there was something that was making them skittish. He was determined to find out what that was. Once he knew, he would report to the King.

As the second guard in command, Mitteran wanted to stay in the King's good graces and always did above and beyond what was expected of him.

He watched a Catling trying to break through the border and suddenly disappear in a puff of smoke. Where did it go? Something strange is going on here. He leaned in closer to take a look but there were only some ashes. As he turned away from the border and planned to report to the King, he saw a light streaming through the air above him and disappearing into the trees of the Unknown Territory. What was that?

There was a smell of something burning in the air. He looked around but did not see anything aflame. He had to hurry to report this phenomenon to the King right away.

Mitteran soon found King Gateskin and called out to him.

King Gateskin looked up when he heard Mitteran's distressed voice.

"What's wrong, Mitteran? Did Spindle tell you that I was looking for you?"

"No, I didn't see Spindle but I think something strange is going on in the UT. I think you need to hear this."

King Gateskin gave his full attention to Mitteran at the sound of his concern. "What is it that has gotten you so worked up, Mitteran?"

The guard explained what he saw.

"That does sound weird. How could a Catling disappear like that without a trace? You said you smelled something burning at that time too?"

"Yes, it was as if the Catling went up in flame without the flames. I looked closer and only saw some ashes."

"That is strange. Thank you for telling me this. We will have to keep watch to make sure the Catlings don't get through. It appears that something is pushing them out of their land or at least frightening them enough to make them try to break through our borders. They wouldn't normally act in that manner."

"Right, I thought of that too, King. It wasn't like them to act fearful of anything or anyone."

"Take a few men with you to keep an eye on the borders. If you see Spindle tell him about this too. Spindle did mention something about a flashing light. I wonder if that is the same thing that you saw. Spindle is also looking for a missing young Sprite. Keep your eyes open for this Sprite. He disappeared earlier today. His parents are worried about him."

"Do you think this light could have something to do with the disappearing Sprite and Catling?"

"Maybe, but we need to keep a lookout. I would like to capture it and see what it is and how dangerous it is. I will contact my Wizards about doing this. No need to worry about this, Mitteran, just keep an eye on the Catlings. I don't want them inside our borders running amuck."

"Yes, of course, King." Mitteran went to find more guards to assist him on the borders and keep an eye out for the missing Sprite and the disappearing beam of light at the same time.

King Gateskin instructed his guards to finish up the huts so he could take care of this new development. He headed over to the Wizards' house to inform them about this beam of light that was flying around.

When he arrived at their hut, they quickly opened the door and welcomed him in. "Good to see you, King. We were planning to visit you about the chest. We think we can open it soon and feel as if it is safe enough now. There is nothing that we can detect there."

"I see. That is good to know. But now we have a problem that sounds quite suspicious. It is a beam of light that is flying around our borders and into the UT."

"A beam of light, you say, King. How large is this beam of light?" Marno, the Head Wizard asked.

"I don't know how large it is. Mitteran just informed me that he saw it overhead near the border of UT and Sovorotskina. But that is not all. He said he saw a Catling trying to break through our borders and that it appeared to be afraid of something. Suddenly it disappeared in front of him."

"Disappeared in front of him? That is strange. There wasn't a Wizard around to do that, was there?"

"Not that I know of. You are the only Wizards that live here."

"And you too, King," Marno added with a grin.

King Gateskin nodded and grinned back at him.

The four Wizards put their heads together and whispered back and forth.

"Will you share what you are whispering? I need to know what you think," King Gateskin stressed.

"Most certainly, King. We were just comparing thoughts so that we could come up with one clear one for you. We think that it is the work of a Wizard or maybe a powerful fairy."

"Where do you think this Wizard or fairy came from?"

"Well, it is quite possible that it escaped out of this chest here. Maybe that is why we don't feel anything inside it anymore. When we first got it from you there was definitely something inside that was keeping it tighter and making it heavier. It is much lighter now. We haven't seen anything come out of it but that doesn't mean that it didn't somehow escape." Marno explained.

"That was my idea, King," Fortag, Wizard second in command, bragged with a wide grin.

"Not completely, Fortag," Tornak and Wassor announced together as they gave their fellow bragging Wizard a frown of disappointment.

"Okay, maybe you both suggested it too. But we could all take the credit for that." Fortag winked at his fellow Wizards.

"Listen, all of you. This is serious. I don't care whose idea it was. We need to find this thing and do something to prevent it from harming anyone else. One lost Catling isn't too important right now but a missing young Sprite is. I need you four to assist in finding this entity of light and destroying it or at least capturing it and putting it safely away until you can discover what it is."

"There is a missing Sprite?" Tornak asked in a surprised voice. "They never get lost."

"Right. They help everyone find their way around the forests. How could he get lost?" Wassor enquired.

"That is for you to find out, Wizards. Now get started and don't stop until you have this light entity in hand or locked away. If you find the Sprite, alert me or my guards right away."

"Yes, King," the Wizards announced in unison as they exchanged worried glances with each other.

"Where do we start, Marno?" Fortag asked the Head Wizard.

"We'll go to the borders where Mitteran saw the Catling disappear. Maybe the boy is close by hiding out."

"Maybe or maybe, he is…." Wassor began to say.

"No, he will not be…" Tornak stated.

"What will we do when we find it, whatever it is?" Fortag asked in a quivering voice.

"What is wrong with you, Fortag?" Marno asked as he gave his fellow Wizard a deep frown of disapproval. "You are a Wizard and should not be afraid of anything."

Fortag shrugged his shoulders and followed the other Wizards out to begin their search.

CHAPTER TWENTY-SIX

King Gateskin bade goodbye to his friend, King Cavelan and his wife Queen Savina, before turning his attention to the latest problems that he had to solve.

"You have your hands full, my friend. Don't worry about us. We don't need an escort to fly home. Let's keep in touch. If you need me, just Conference Call me," Cavelan said.

"I will, Cavelan. Thank you for stopping by. Did Solinara give you something to eat?"

"Of course. She is the epitome of the perfect hostess. I ate too many of her cookies and meat turnovers already. Thank you for everything. I hope these dragons work out for you and that all the rest of the problems can be solved."

Queen Solinara threw Cavelan a kiss in thanks for his kind words as she gave Queen Savina another tight hug and whispered that they would talk soon.

"Thanks, Cavelan. I will handle whatever there is to handle. Take care and safe travels, my friend," Gateskin said.

King Gateskin turned his attention to the issues at hand. He was worried about the safety of all of Sovorotskina after hearing about the disappearing Catling. He didn't care about the Catling as such but did care about the missing Sprite. He feared that something happened to the young Sprite. He couldn't bear to have to tell the parents that fact.

Spindle was scouting all the areas inside the UT with the other Sprites in search of the young Sprite. There was no sign of him but they did notice that there were fewer Catlings roaming around. The ones that did roam appeared nervous and were hiding in their dens or amongst heavy bushes.

That wasn't right. These Catlings commanded the UT and nothing was bigger or scarier than they were. What could be making them so fearful?

Suddenly one of the Sprites cried out in alarm. "Look up there! What is that light?"

Spindle flew over to the Sprite who had alerted them. "Don't get near it. We don't know what it is. It could be dangerous and the reason why the Catlings are so nervous."

"How could a beam of light hurt them?" one Sprite asked.

"I don't know but we can't take the chance to get too close to it. I will report this to King Gateskin. He will know what to do."

Spindle told the other Sprites, "Be watchful and keep a distance away from the light. I will return shortly."

As Spindle flew back to see the King, he noticed the four Wizards flying around near the borders. What were they doing there?

He flew down closer to them to ask. "What are you doing here?"

"Hi Spindle. We are on a mission for the King," answered Marno.

"Hmm, I see. Are you looking for a beam of light by any chance?"

"Why yes, we are? How did you know?" Tornak questioned in surprise.

"Well, I just found it. It's in the UT. I was on my way back to see King Gateskin to let him know I found it."

"He told you to find it?" Fortag asked in surprise.

"He also told us to find it," Wassor announced.

"Well, I found it and now what are you going to do about catching it? I can't catch it since I am not a Wizard," Spindle stated.

"That is our job. Go tell the King that we will capture it," Marno said.

"I am on my way. Be careful. We have no idea what it is capable of," Spindle warned.

"Of course. We are always careful, aren't we?" Fortag asked as he looked at the other Wizards.

Marno grunted at Fortag and shook his head. "Stop being so negative! We have a job to do and it will get done. Pull out your wands and prepare to use the spells we had rehearsed over the chest. One of them is bound to work."

"What if they don't work?" Wassor asked, warily.

"They will," Marno exclaimed, which silenced the others.

They waved their wands around as they walked further into the UT keeping alert for any Catlings who might be there.

"That is strange. There are no Catlings around. Where are they?" Tornak asked, as he looked around carefully.

"I don't know. Maybe they are hiding out, afraid of this beam of light," Wassor said.

"Look over there," Fortag exclaimed. "What is that thing on top of the high branch in that tree?"

"It's a Sprite but it is too small," Marno stated.

"It looks like a young Sprite. It is quite small though as if it shrunk," Tornak said as he squinted to look closer.

"Let me get it down from the tree. I will use a spell to bring it here," Marno said.

As the thing was brought out of the tree it looked like a tiny Sprite, tinier than any they had ever seen.

The Sprite opened his eyes and looked at them. "Is it gone?"

"What is gone?" Marno asked the Sprite.

"The beam of light. It made me shrink. I may never grow bigger again. Can you help me grow?" he asked the Wizards.

"Let's get you home and away from here. We will work on a spell to do that. Don't worry, little Sprite," Marno said in a calm manner.

"Thank you so much, Wizard. I was afraid to move. Are you sure it is gone?"

"Yes, we saw it fly deeper into the UT. We will capture it and make sure it doesn't harm anyone else."

"Thank you. I can manage to fly home from tree to tree as long as you keep watch for that light. I don't want it to follow me."

"No worries. Go quickly and don't look back. We will keep watch," Marno stated as he smiled at the frightened Sprite.

The Wizards watched the Sprite fly from tree to tree and disappear from view. They turned their attention back to the beam of light that they could see far off in the distance. It was flying around in the high treetops.

More Sprites were calling out a warning to the other Sprites about this thing that kept flying into their tree huts. It was being a nuisance.

The Wizards called out to the Sprites, "What is going on?"

The Sprites answered back, "We don't know what this thing is but that it is getting into all our huts and causing a disturbance. It keeps tossing things around as if it is looking for something."

"Stay out of its way. We are coming to capture it," Marno announced as they flew up to the tree where the beam could be seen inside one of the Sprites' huts.

The Wizards waved their wands simultaneously and recited a spell to capture it inside a small box they had brought with them.

The beam kept dimming and going out as they kept the chant going until it lit up brightly and disappeared inside their box.

"We did it!" exclaimed Fortag.

Marno nodded and said, "Yes, I think we did. Now we must hurry back and tell the King we completed our assignment. He will be pleased."

"We also need to report that we found the missing Sprite," Wassor reminded.

CHAPTER TWENTY-SEVEN

Spindle intercepted the shrunken Sprite who was flying through the trees toward his home. He stopped the shaken Sprite to ask what had happened to him.

"Please take a minute to calm down. You are not in danger now. I will protect you. What happened to you?"

The miniature Sprite shook all over and began to explain to Spindle, "I was roaming around in the UT and stumbled on a bright light that was in the treetops. I stopped to get a closer look but before I could get a good look at it, I found myself like this. The light had somehow shrunken me. Look at me! No one will know who I am or even see me because I am so small." The Sprite began to sob so hard that he began to shake all over.

"Wait a minute, little guy. I will help you. I think I know how we can bring you back to your former size. Come with me."

The little Sprite nodded and stopped his tears as he followed Spindle.

The two Sprites arrived at King Gateskin's home and waited at the door until someone answered their knocks.

While they were waiting, Spindle said that he would send a message to the Sprite's parents that he was safe and well and would be home soon.

"Thank you for doing that, Spindle. I didn't want to go home looking like this. It could give my parents a heart attack if they saw me. They are getting up in years, you know, almost 200 years old."

Spindle chuckled at this and patted the Sprite on his miniature head.

The door was opened by Queen Solinara who looked up at the two Sprites who were flitting around in the air. "Well, this is a surprise, Spindle. I didn't know you had a fellow Sprite this small."

"Yes, unfortunately, I need to explain. Is King Gateskin here?"

"No, I think he is still with the dragons."

"Yes, that's right. He did tell me he would be doing the training most of the day. Well, I will go find him to help me."

"Wait a minute, Spindle. What did you need for him to do? Maybe I can help you," Queen Solinara said as she looked at the sad tiny Sprite.

"Oh, can you? That would be most helpful, Queen Solinara," the tiny Sprite stated with a bow.

"Of course, please come in and I will see what I can do."

Spindle lifted the Sprite onto his shoulder and flew into the Queen's kitchen to sit at the table.

"Now explain what happened to you first of all. Thereafter I will be able to determine what kind of magic it took to do this."

"Do you think it was some kind of Dark Magic, Queen?" the miniature Sprite asked.

"I don't know yet until you explain what happened to you."

"I see, of course." The tiny Sprite began to explain what he had already told Spindle about his strange encounter.

"Hmm. That is quite odd. A beam of light you say. I wonder what it could be and where it came from," the Queen mused.

The two Sprites waited patiently while Queen Solinara gathered some herbs and pulled out her book of spells.

Before the Queen could begin a spell on the Sprite someone else knocked at her door. She moved to the door and opened it. There stood the four Wizards wearing broad smiles and a small box in the Head Wizard's hand.

"Well, this is a pleasant surprise to see all four of you here. What brings you by today? Is everything okay?"

"Oh yes, Queen Solinara. Everything is just perfect. We need to see the King right away. We have urgent news for him."

"Urgent news about what, may I ask?"

"Well, the King gave us a mission and we have completed said mission satisfactorily," Marno announced with an expression of pride on his face.

"That is good to hear, but King Gateskin is not here. He is with the dragons."

"Oh, okay. We can wait or come back later," Marno said.

Spindle was listening to the interchange and flew over to the doorway to peek at the Wizards. He asked, "Do you, by any chance, have the beam in that box?"

"Why yes, we do, Spindle."

"I'm glad you caught it. King Gateskin will be happy to hear you did that. The King also told me about a missing Sprite."

"We heard about the missing Sprite. We found him and sent him home," Fortag announced.

"Oh, you did? Thank you for doing that. The tiny Sprite is here now."

When the miniature Sprite heard them talking about him, he came to the door and flew up so the Wizards could see him.

"I am here. Thank you, Wizards, for saving me from that light. If you hadn't come, it might have reduced me to ashes." The Sprite shivered at his own words.

"No problem, baby Sprite. It was our pleasure," Wassor replied.

"I am not a baby, Wizard!" the tiny Sprite exclaimed with a frown on his brown face.

"So sorry. I did not want to insult you, but you are quite small even for a Sprite," Wasson continued.

"Please come in and we can discuss this further and maybe find a solution together for this dear little Sprites' dilemma," Queen Solinara explained.

The Wizards walked into the kitchen and sat around the table at the Queen's request. Marno held the box tightly in his hands.

They discussed the solutions and which spells might work for the poor Sprite who waited with wide-eyed wonder and hope.

CHAPTER TWENTY-EIGHT

King Gateskin and his guards completed the huts for the wolves and saved some of the leftover lumber for future projects. Gateskin went back to see the dragons and Aharona and Navaeha.

"King Gateskin, I wondered if you would be coming back here. Were our dragons successful in finding enough lumber for your huts?"

"Yes, in fact, they brought back more than enough. I will save some for future projects. I came back to see how the dragons are doing. Are they still arguing?"

"No, they appear to be quiet now. I sent our two dragons into the lair to check on them," Aharona explained.

"Maybe I should go see them myself and let them know that I am patient and will wait for their final decision about staying here in the two weeks' time. That should be enough for them to figure out what they can agree on."

"Hopefully it will be, King," Navaeha said. "After all, we only have less than two weeks' time now."

King Gateskin nodded in agreement and headed back to the lair. He peeked in and saw the four dragons sleeping in separate stalls. It was peaceful for now. He tiptoed out but not before he heard the voice of Callum.

"King, all is good here. No worries. We will keep an eye on these two. They seemed to be all out of arguments for the time being. We did try to convince them that this is the perfect place to live. We would love to live here too if our mistresses allowed that to happen."

King Gateskin's eyes grew wide at the dragon's surprising words. "I don't think your mistresses would want to live here. They would miss their parents and friends back on Dragonaria."

"Maybe or maybe not," Callum added as he blew out a smoke ring. "It's something to muse about later, King. I need to go back to sleep now. Talk to you later."

Gateskin watched the dragon go right back to sleep as if he never woke up. I wish I could sleep as soundly as that, he whispered to himself.

Aharona and Navaeha watched the King come out of the lair shaking his head.

"Is everything okay, King?" Aharona asked.

"Yes, but Callum just said something quite surprising."

"What was that?" Aharona's curiosity was piqued. "I hope he was not disrespectful in any way."

"Oh, no, not at all. He is always respectful to me and my family. Both of your dragons are well behaved and always polite. You should be proud of the wonderful job you have done with them."

"Thank you, King Gateskin. We appreciate your kind words," Navaeha said.

"But what did Callum say to you?" Aharona urged.

"Well, he said he and Evander would like to live here. They evidently discussed how special it is to be able to live here with the other two dragons. They were doing their best to convince them to stay with us."

"They did? They want to live here with you? Don't they like us anymore?" Aharona stated with a disgruntled look.

"That's not it at all. I think they were just trying to state that this is a nice place for the two dragons to live instead of on Dragonaria."

"That sounds like they really believe this place to be better for them too," Aharona said with a shocked expression.

"I can't believe it either, sister," Navaeha stated. "What if we moved here permanently?"

"What? You want to live here and not in Dragonaria with our parents and friends?" Aharona asked, incredulous.

"Well, it is a beautiful place to be and we always feel at home when we are here. I think we could adjust and so would our parents if they didn't see us all the time. We could visit them from time to time," Navaeha continued.

"I don't think this is a good idea to even consider, Navaeha. We couldn't leave our parents to try to fend off Elowen. She is too dangerous and our parents are not getting any younger."

"I know but it was just a thought, sister. Let's not get angry about it. I only made a suggestion as Callum had done. It is forgotten for now. Let's go take a rest ourselves."

"Ladies, please don't be upset about this. Callum was only stating something in jest. I don't think he really meant it. Besides he is trying to be the one to keep the other dragons in line for me. I appreciate that. I did thank him and Evander profusely for bringing all the lumber here and gave them both a treat which they gobbled up quickly. I can't tell you enough how helpful you and your dragons have been since you came to us."

"Thank you, King. We are happy to help in any way we can. We do like it here too," Aharona said.

"I'm glad to hear that, Aharona. I thought maybe you weren't as happy as your sister and your dragons."

"Not at all, I just worry about our parents and our sister. They can't protect themselves. They don't have magic like Elowen does or like you and your family do. That's the good kind of magic, not Dark Magic like Elowen's," Aharona stressed.

"I understand. Why don't you come back to my home now where you have a place to rest. The dragons are all settled and I will have my children bring them more food soon. I'm sure you are both hungry and tired. My wife is probably wondering where we are by now."

King Gateskin led the ladies back to his house not knowing what was transpiring there.

***

When the threesome arrived at the King's home, he was startled to see how many were sitting at his dining room table with their heads close together.

"What's going on here?"

Queen Solinara raised her head when she heard her husband's voice. "Oh dear, you are just in time to help us." She explained what they were trying to do for the tiny Sprite.

"You found him? That's good news. Do his parents know that he is okay?"

"Yes King, I sent them a message," Spindle spoke up.

"Also, we were the ones to find him, King Gateskin," Marno announced.

"Ah, that is good but what about the beam of light? Did you find that too?"

"Yes, we did, King. It is here in this box. We trapped it with a chant," Marno explained.

"Very good news indeed. Now what are we going to do with it?"

"We came here to discuss that with you, King," Marno stated.

"What do you think it is? Does it have power?"

"Yes, it definitely has some kind of power since it made this poor Sprite shrink."

"I see. It is quite small. Are you all right, little one?" King Gateskin bent down to ask the Sprite.

"Yes, King. I am fine, just much smaller than I ever was."

"Well, we will see what we can do to change that, little guy. Don't worry."

The tiny Sprite nodded and tried to smile at the King's words.

"What have you come up with so far, Solinara?"

"Well, I have several spells that may help but I don't know if we can get him to be exactly as he was. He may be a little smaller or maybe a little bigger when we are through."

"I don't mind being a little bigger. It's better than being a little smaller. I was already small for my age," the tiny Sprite stated.

"Let's look over the spells and maybe we can combine two together to make him the best he can be," King Gateskin said as he smiled at the nervous Sprite.

Queen Solinara looked up to see Aharona and Navaeha standing there. She apologized for all the confusion, escorted the dragon ladies to their rooms and said she would send one of her children there with refreshments soon.

Solinara called out to Serena and told her what to bring to the ladies so she could go back to solving the problem for the poor Sprite.

CHAPTER TWENTY-NINE

The dragon ladies nodded to the Queen and listened as the King and others worked together to get the right spell to fix the poor little Sprite. The dragon ladies excused themselves and went into their rooms to wait for their food and to rest so they wouldn't be in the way.

Once their heads hit their pillows, they were out cold and didn't hear anything that was going on out in the dining room.

When Serena came in with their food, she placed it on their nightstands with covers to keep them warm and tiptoed out of the room.

***

Queen Solinara used two of her spells together, a Transformation Spell and another one that she had never used before to make something grow larger. She would call it a Sprite Spell named after the little Sprite if it worked. Time would tell.

The Sprite was trembling as they chanted the new spells over him. He tried to stand as still as he could and waited for something to happen. He kept looking down at his feet and hands to see if they were growing.

"Don't think about anything, Sprite. It will work soon. Just try to relax as we continue to spread the spells over you," Queen Solinara explained.

They all watched the Sprite for several minutes to see if he was growing, but nothing happened.

The Wizards suggested that they could add another chant to speed up the process if the Queen wanted some assistance.

"What do you have to add, Wizards?" she asked.

"Well, we have done a few things in the past when we were in Parotovina for the King. He wanted to enlarge some of the vegetables in their garden. This spell we tried did help make them a little larger," Marno stated.

"Okay, but we can't put in too much or he will grow too fast and too big," King Gateskin said.

"Let's just try one dash of our spell to two dashes of yours, Queen. That should work," Marno continued with a wave of his hands after putting the box on the table.

What everyone didn't see was the box was moving closer to the Sprite. When the box was right next to the Sprite it lit up and shook.

The Wizards stopped waving their hands and grabbed the box but couldn't touch it for it was too hot.

"What is happening here?" Marno exclaimed in alarm.

"Let me pick up the box, Marno," King Gateskin announced as he covered his hands with a spell that would prevent him from getting burned.

"I think it is trying to escape, King," Marno announced.

"It may be doing that or maybe it is trying to help us fix the Sprite since it did the shrinking to begin with," the King explained.

"Wait a minute. Look at the chest. It is getting brighter," Fortag stated in panic mode.

The Sprite cried out, "I am growing now! Look at me! I am larger than I was before!"

"Yes, he is. But he is not stopping. He is still growing. We must stop him from growing too large," Queen Solinara stated in dismay.

King Gateskin covered the box snuffing out the light and the Sprite stopped growing.

"I am just the right size now. I am bigger than I was before but not too big," the happy Sprite said with a broad smile.

"Yes, I think you are just the right size, Sprite. You are almost my size now," Spindle said.

"Thank you all so much! I can't wait to show my parents that I am bigger now. They always called me small fry. Now I will no longer have that name," the Sprite giggled.

King Gateskin spoke to Spindle, "Can you escort this large Sprite home? I think his parents are probably wondering why he didn't come home yet."

"Sure thing, King. Let's go, Big Fry!" Spindle patted the larger Sprite on his shoulder and they flew out together through the opened window.

"Well, now that the Sprite is back to normal, we need to take care of this beam of light," King Gateskin announced.

"Do you want us to take it back to our house and work on it, King?" Marno asked.

"Yes, I think that would be a good idea. Keep it locked up inside a safe place so it can't get out. This box is not good enough to do that."

"Of course, King. We have a safe that will do just that. We will lock it up."

"Let me know what you find out about it. If it is Dark Magic or not and what is it capable of. We now know that it can shrink or grow things."

Mitteran arrived at the King's door and was about to knock when it was opened by the Wizards who were on their way out.

"Oops, sorry. I came to see the King."

"Mitteran, come in. The Wizards are just leaving. What did you find out about the Catlings?"

"Well, I wanted to let you know that whatever that beam of light is, it is definitely dangerous. As I already told you, I witnessed what it can do."

King Gateskin turned to the Wizards and said, "You should hear this. Mitteran already reported this to me."

"What did it do?" Marno, the Head Wizard, asked as Mitteran took a seat.

"One of the Catlings came to the border but didn't stop. It tried to break through the spell you put there. When it couldn't break through it suddenly burst into flame, but there was no fire, just ashes left."

"That is strange. There was no fire?" Marno inquired.

"No, it was almost as if something made it disappear in midair in a puff of smoke. I could smell something burning though. I thoroughly checked all the borders but didn't see any more Catlings close by," Mitteran continued.

"Yes, I think there are fewer Catlings all of a sudden. This beam of light must have had something to do with that. The dragons said they didn't see too many over there either when they went to the UT to retrieve some fallen limbs for me to build the wolves' huts," King Gateskin explained.

"I don't like the sound of this," Marno stated with a wary expression that he shared with his fellow Wizards.

"We need to keep an eye out for any more problems caused by this beam of light. We don't know how long it has been out and about," King Gateskin warned.

CHAPTER THIRTY

Spindle was once again scouting around for any problems at the borders. He knew that Mitteran had already checked the borders with some other guards but he felt better checking the borders once more himself.

He first planned to check on the Quintaroons and see if they needed to take a stroll.

The two Quintaroons were once the creations of Queen Beregina from Parotovina using her Dark Magic. She had created them by turning two men who were vagabonds into these strange and dangerous creatures. King Kaposkaran had used them to invade Sovorotskina and cause havoc to King Gateskin and report back to him. Instead, what happened was, they were turned back to men by King Gateskin and his wizards to take up residence in Sovorotskina, never to return to Parotovina where they would be punished for not doing their assignments. They swore loyalty to King Gateskin in return for his protection.

Spindle knocked at their door and waited to hear any movement. He unlocked the door and walked in. The room was dark and there was no sign of the two Quintaroons. He called out, "Quintal, Talon, where are you?"

The two Quintaroons came out of the bathing room.

"What were you doing?"

"We were just trying to…," Talon began.

"Ssh, never mind, Spindle. We had to wash up, that's all," Quintal responded.

Spindle looked at them closely and waited a minute to see if they had anything else to add.

"Do you want to go out and get some fresh air?"

"Yes, most definitely!" they exclaimed together.

"Are you ready to go?" Spindle asked as he flitted over their heads.

"We are ready. Aren't we?" Quintal looked at Talon and gave him a meaningful stare.

Talon nodded and said, "Yep, we're ready."

Spindle was aware that something was going on between these two characters. He didn't trust them for a minute. He would have to keep them in close rein.

While Spindle was flying overhead keeping his eyes on the two Quintaroons, he surveyed the area all around.

The two Quintaroons whispered back and forth to each other and avoided looking at Spindle who was flying above them.

"We are not going in the right direction of the dragons' lair. I want to see them," Quintal stated as he kept looking up at the Sprite.

Talon responded, "We will have to try to turn around quickly forcing Spindle to follow us. "What do you plan to do when we get there?"

"I don't know what I want to do, I am just curious about these creatures," Quintal said.

"They are dangerous, Quintal," Talon warned.

Spindle could hear some of what the Quintaroons were saying but he didn't catch what Talon had said to Quintal. All he knew was that they were intrigued by the dragons and wanted to go see them. He would let the man-creatures lead the way but would control what they did before they could get themselves killed. Spindle wasn't too sure about the female dragon and knew that she could get riled up easily if her naps were disrupted.

The Quintaroons turned around and began heading toward the dragons' lair. They tried to do it in a sneaky way by saying, "Oh, look over there! What is that?"

Spindle was wise to their wily ways and did not fall for this. Instead, he led the way to the dragons' lair and said, "Well, if you really want to say 'hello' to our new dragons; let's go."

Quintal and Talon looked up at Spindle with shocked expressions. "You are going to let us see them?" Talon asked.

"Yes, why not? But I must warn you. They may be sleeping and have not eaten since breakfast and could be hungry for two Quintaroons who are posing as men."

Talon stopped in his tracks before reaching the lair and shook his head at Quintal. "I think I changed my mind about seeing the dragons.

Why don't we wait until after they have eaten something?"

"Are you sure about that?" Spindle pressed as he prepared to open the door to the lair.

"No, please don't open the door. We can come back another time," Talon stressed in a shaky voice.

Quintal nodded in agreement but looked up suddenly to see the door to the lair open.

Out stepped two dragons who were yawning and stretching their wings causing a wind to blow over them.

Madrigal looked down at the two men who were staring at them with their mouths open and asked, "Who are you?"

Spindle laughed at the expressions of shock on the Quintaroon-men's faces. He winked at the dragons at the same time.

Izara bent down and looked closely at the men and said, "They look like they are tasty enough to eat. Don't you think so, Madrigal?"

Madrigal answered by smacking his lips causing drool to land at the feet of the frightened men.

Talon grabbed Quintal's hand and pulled him away as fast as he could. They ran all the way to their house and never looked back.

Spindle winked at the dragons again and said, "Thanks. I couldn't have done a better job of frightening them enough to stay away from you. You did my job. Now I won't have to walk them back home. I'm sure they have locked the door and barred it with furniture," he chuckled.

"Who are they anyway?" Izara asked.

Spindle didn't want to share the whole truth with them but said, "They are former Parotovinans who sought refuge from their ruler who threatened their lives if they returned."

"Hmm, I see," Madrigal responded.

"Does that mean that no one would miss them if we ate them?" Izara asked with a wide grin.

"Really, Izara? We are not to eat anything other than what the King and his family provide for us."

"I think that is a good way to think of it, Madrigal," Spindle stated.

"Speaking of food, where is our meal?" Izara asked as she flew up to look toward the King's home.

"I will check on that for you. Stay here and out of trouble. What you can do is keep an eye out for any Catlings who are trying to break through the barriers. If you see any, please call out to me right away."

"Sure, we can do that for you, Spindle. Don't forget our food though," Madrigal added.

Spindle nodded to them and flew over to the Quintaroons' house to lock their door from the outside to ensure they could not get out. The Sprite did not have the ability to use a spell to lock it. The King have given him a key to use whenever he had to take the creatures out for a walk.

Izara flew up to look at the borders hoping to spot a wayward Catling.

Madrigal did the same but kept an eye also on his mate to ensure that she did not venture too far into the UT.

CHAPTER THIRTY-ONE

From the UT something was watching the dragons as they flew over the borders between UT and Sovorotskina. It did not like the dragons getting too close to it. It had finally found a safe place to hide and didn't want to be disturbed. It had already destroyed some of the noisy Catlings who tried to get too close to it.

This beam of light was waiting for word from the original Wizard that had put it into the chest with magic many years before. It has been waiting a long time and was tired of being held captive. It was waiting for someone to allow it to do what it was capable of doing. It would take the original Wizard or another powerful one to contain it. Until that time, it would watch everything around it.

This beam managed to split away from itself before the Wizards captured it and took it away. It could keep doing this and become many beams of light that could cause much damage to anything that came in its way. The only thing that happened each time it split itself was that its clones were not as powerful as it was when it was whole.

Izara swooped down to get a closer look at the UT border and roared as something singed the tip of her left wing. She called out to Madrigal to help her find out what did this.

"What's wrong, Izara?" Madrigal came to her side to inspect her injured wing. "What did that to you?"

Izara looked down at the border and noticed a beam of light there. She pointed to it and alerted Madrigal. "Watch out! See that beam of light. That is what the King was searching for."

"I think the Wizards got it already. What is this, another one?"

"I'm afraid it is, Madrigal. It hurt me! Can you please blow on it and put out the fire. It feels as if it is still in flames."

"There is no fire there, Izara, but I will do all I can to calm it down. Let's get back to our lair. I will fix it for you. We should tell the King. He will need to send the Wizards there to capture this second beam of light before it harms anyone else."

"I really don't care about anyone else right now, Madrigal. Just take care of me, okay?"

"No worries, my love. I will take care of you first and afterward I will report to the King. We don't want this to happen to you again the next time you get too curious about the Catlings."

"I wasn't being too curious, Mad. I was just doing what Spindle asked us to do so we could get our lunch. Where is that Sprite with our lunch, by the way?"

"Don't worry about that, Izzy! Let's get back to our lair. You will be safe there."

"I'm not afraid if that is what you are implying, Mad! I am not afraid of anything."

"I know, Izzy. I know. You are a brave dragon. That's why I love you."

"You love me? You never said that before, Mad."

"Didn't I?" Madrigal chuckled, knowing that his words always softened the edges of his mate's ire.

***

Spindle was relating the episode of the Quintaroons and dragons with King Gateskin and also mentioned that the dragons were hungry and getting antsy.

"Thank you, Spindle, for keeping an eye on both the Quintaroons and the dragons. I will let Solinara know about the food. She will have the children bring it right away to the dragons. I don't want them to go looking for other sources of food."

"I don't think we will have any problems with the dragons. Madrigal can keep Izara in line. He has quite a good sense of humor too."

"Yes, I agree, Spindle. He certainly does have a sense of humor. If only his mate was as easy to handle," Gateskin sighed. "I can see that Madrigal can handle Izara for us."

"Well, I better get back to the dragons. They are keeping an eye out on the borders for any Catlings that may be trying to get in. Also, I need to tell them that their lunch is on its way."

"Yes, please do that. Thanks, Spindle."

Just as Spindle flew away to relay the message to the hungry dragons, the three Wizards flew by him and over to see the King.

King Gateskin stopped in his tracks as he was ready to open the door to his home when he spied the Wizards' disgruntled expressions. They were holding the chest tight against them.

"Is there a problem, Wizards?" King Gateskin enquired.

"We need to explain what has happened to the beam of light. Can we come in and sit down with you. We may have to come up with a plan."

"Come in please, and sit down."

The Wizards settled down at the table and placed the chest between them keeping their hands over it protecting it for some reason.

"Why are you holding the chest like that between you?"

The Head Wizard began to explain, "We noticed when we got back home that there was a hole in the side of the chest. We think that some of the beams of light may have escaped."

"Escaped? How could that be?"

"I'm sorry, King. We will do all we can to find it. We need to keep everyone inside until we do. This beam of light has powers. We do not know everything except that it can burn things and change them like the Catlings and the little Sprite."

"Yes, I agree. It is quite possibly capable of much more than we imagined. If it can split itself, we need to keep everyone safe. We don't know where it is. It could be right at my back door."

Queen Solinara received her husband's urgent message to get the children inside right away.

She messaged him back, "The children are flying over to feed the dragons."

"I will go there and make sure they are safe. Check all the wolves and the animals in the barn. Close the barn door and get back inside as soon as you can. I will bring the children back safely."

The Wizards followed the King to the dragons' lair.

CHAPTER THIRTY-TWO

Spindle found the dragons inside their lair. He could hear moaning. He called out to them. "Are you all right?"

Callum and Evander stood nearby to give Izara some sympathy.

"No, Spindle. Izara had a mishap," Madrigal explained what had happened to his mate and how he was taking care of her.

"I'm sorry to hear that, Izara. I had no idea that the beam of light was still out there. The Wizards were supposed to capture it. I don't know how this could be another beam of light."

"I don't understand it either. Izara is doing better. I caused a wind around her wing to calm down the pain of the burn. This beam is strong and can deliver some serious burns."

"I will tell the King about this. The Queen has spells and medicine to handle all kinds of injuries, especially burns. I will return shortly."

As Spindle flew back to the King's home, he saw the King and the Wizards heading his way. He stopped in mid-flight to meet them.

"I was just going to see you, King," Spindle began to explain. "The dragons need some medicine for a serious burn. It appears that there is another beam of light somewhere in the UT."

"Yes, we know about that. In the UT, you say?" King Gateskin asked.

"Yes, that is where Izara said she saw the light and it burned the tip of her left wing."

"Go see the Queen, Spindle. Tell her what you said about the dragons. She will come with medicine. Did you see my children at the lair?"

"No, but I was in such a hurry. I could have missed them along the way. They must be on their way there now."

The King looked around and sent a message to his oldest daughter, Serena. "Where are you?"

Serena stopped filling the large bowls and answered. "We are with the dragon ladies in Mother's workshop. We are on our way to feed the other two dragons shortly."

"Don't come this way. Stay home. I will bring the food to the other dragons. It is too dangerous to be out and about. I will explain later. Get yourself and your siblings home right now."

"Okay, Father. But I don't understand," Serena said as she shrugged her shoulders and called her siblings to get inside their house per their father's request, leaving the tubs of food half full for their mother to finish.

Solinara messaged her husband and said, "I will bring the food to the dragons and make sure the children are safely back inside."

The dragon ladies left the workshop and returned to the lair to see what was happening. They wanted to aid in any way they could.

Spindle found the Queen in her workshop preparing more food for the dragons. He explained what he needed from her and flew away.

Solinara finished filling the tubs full of the fresh food she had made for the dragons and putting a spell on them, lifted them up into the air directing them to the dragons' lair while she quickly gathered her herbs and was right behind Spindle. The Queen had some spells in mind to try on the dragon's burn. They would have to be more powerful to work on a dragon.

***

Serena and her siblings whispered between each other. "What is going on? Are the dragons causing trouble? Or are the Catlings getting inside the borders again?"

"I have no idea," Serena said, to calm her brother and sister down.

"What are we going to do? We can't just sit here?" Simon stressed as he paced back and forth.

"We need to do something! Father and Mother could be in danger from whatever it is," Catalina stated with furrowed brow.

"Spindle could be in danger too!" Serena cried out in alarm.

"He could be shrunk like the other Sprite. That wouldn't be a good thing, Serena. He is already smaller than you," Simon added.

Serena met her brother with a stern expression meant to quiet his retorts.

"Sorry, Serena. He didn't mean anything by that. We do know how much you and Spindle like each other," Catalina stated with a sad face.

"I think Spindle can take care of himself unlike that other Sprite. He has powers that some of the Sprites do not have," Serena bragged.

"So, you don't have to worry about him after all," Simon responded in a soft voice.

"I will send a message to Mother and see what is going on. She always knows what Father is up to," Serena said as she waited to hear back from their mother.

"Just stay inside, Serena. I am at the dragons' lair tending to the injured dragon. Nothing for you to concern yourself with at the moment. I will explain more when I know more. Take care of your brother and sister and fix them something. They must be hungry. I didn't get to do that before I rushed off," her mother responded.

"Injured dragon? Which one? What happened?" Serena plied her mother with more questions.

"Let me do my nursing and I will get right back to you. Be patient, dear."

"Okay, Mother. I will have more questions when you get here."

"I'm sure you will, Serena."

Serena explained what she could to Simon and Catalina who threw questions at her non-stop.

"Wait a minute, you two. I don't have any answers. We have to wait for Mother to return. We can ask her everything at that time."

"What about the dragon ladies? Did they leave to help?" Simon asked.

"I guess they must have because they aren't around now." Serena stated.

"What if one of the dragons dies?" Catalina exclaimed in alarm.

"Don't think like that, Catalina. We don't know what is happening. Let's make some sandwiches and we can discuss this more. Okay?" Serena tried to calm her sister's fears which she was feeling too.

"I'm hungry. I can eat," Simon announced.

Catalina gave her brother a frown, "You can always eat!"

CHAPTER THIRTY-THREE

"Serena, can't you listen in to Mother and Father's conversations? I know you did that before," Catalina beseeched.

"Yes, I can but I got into trouble last time I did that. Don't you remember? I promised I would never do that again unless…"

"Unless what?" Simon pressed.

"Well, if there was an emergency and one of us was in danger, I could do that."

"This is the time that we may be in danger, Serena," Catalina stated with a frown.

"Not really, Catalina. We are safe here until our parents return. Please eat your lunch and we can play a game to keep your mind off of all of this. They should be back soon."

"What if we summon Uncle Hotenfaran and Aunt Procelina? We can say we miss seeing them. They have been traveling from time to time across Noella Province and haven't stopped by for a visit for a little while. Well at least not since Uncle Hotenfaran was by to help Mother make the dragons' food. Also, we haven't visited with their son, Arubane, for a long time either."

"That's a great idea, Serena. Let's do it. We can share that we are in the dark about something happening here that could put us in danger," Simon grinned.

Before Serena could send a message to her uncle and aunt, the door opened and her parents stood there looking at them.

"Are you all right?" Serena asked them.

"We are fine. But we need to speak with you about what has transpired," their father announced.

"Sit down. Are you finished with your lunch?"

"Yes, we are, Father. I will clear the plates off the table," Serena said with a look of concern.

"Okay, it has come to our attention again that there may be multiple beams of light that are flitting around the village and into the UT. We learned that a part of the original beam that was housed in the chest that we found with the help of the dragons may have split off and escaped. The Wizards captured one of the beams and another was spotted. The Wizards are in the process of looking for more. Once they find them all we will be safe once again."

"How could this happen, Father?" Simon queried.

"We don't know exactly but it appears that this beam of light is capable of splitting itself. We have no idea how many times it has done this or how many more times it will do this again."

"Oh, Father! What can we do to help you?" Catalina cried out in alarm.

"What about the villagers? Are they in danger too?" Simon asked.

"You need not worry about that. It is being taken care of. I have warned the villagers to stay inside as I have you."

"What happened to the dragon? You said that a dragon was injured, Mother." Serena asked with concern.

"Izara was injured when she went too close to one of the beams of light in the UT. She was patrolling the borders for Spindle."

"She obeyed Spindle?" Serena asked in surprise. "Is she okay now?"

"Believe it or not, she did obey him. I think she is getting used to us just don't tell her that," Gateskin chuckled, and got serious once again.

Solinara answered, "Yes, Izara is doing better now after I applied a salve to her burned wing and cast a spell over it to keep it from hurting her so she can rest."

"That's a relief, Mother. When can we go see her?" Serena inquired with a sigh.

"Not yet. Maybe in a day or two," Solinara responded.

"What are we to do, Father? Can we go outside safely?" Simon asked.

"Not yet, son. I need confirmation from the Wizards that they have all of the beams safely locked away."

"What if they keep escaping and splitting?" Serena exclaimed.

"We will deal with that if that happens. I think there may only be one left out there. Now when you must go out, you will not go out without one of us. Do you understand?" Gateskin stated in a strong tone.

"Of course, Father. We will go with either you or Mother. We understand," Serena stressed as she looked at her brother and sister who nodded in agreement.

"Good. Now we need to make sure that all the animals are doing well. Go with your mother to her workshop to gather some food for the wolves. They are hungry and need to eat more than a few times a day."

"Yes, Father," Serena agreed.

Gateskin went outside and looked around. He called Spindle to clarify about anything he may have found.

He messaged the Wizards to keep him informed about the beams of light that may still be around.

Gateskin quickly received a message from the Wizards. "All is quiet here now. We got the last beam of light and they are safely locked away in the repaired chest in our iron safe. We reinforced the wall safely with a few spells that should keep the beams contained. We will keep you informed, King. We plan to do some experimenting on the beams soon. We want to let them settle down for now."

"Thank you, Marno. I appreciate that you are keeping on top of this. I don't want anyone else to be harmed by these pesky beams."

"No problem, King. We have them contained and will keep an eye out for any disturbances these beams may have caused while they were out and about."

"Good man. Who knows what they might have done while they were unattended."

CHAPTER THIRTY-FOUR

In the UT several Catlings were coming out of hiding now that the beams of light were gone. They looked around wary of what could still be lurking in the woods to kill them.

Up to this time they didn't have any enemies or other creatures who were strong enough to threaten or kill them until now.

The Catlings had been thinned out. It was time to procreate again to replenish their numbers. Many of the females were already pregnant prior to the slaughtering of their ranks and would soon deliver their offspring.

The Catlings' ears picked up voices coming their way and the creatures scattered to their dens to watch as some new intruders came through their land.

King Parotovina's men were unaware that they were being watched as they noisily passed through the UT. They felt safe since they had not spotted one of those cat-like creatures that they had heard about from the villagers who had traveled and managed to return after surviving an attack.

One Parotovinan shivered and turned to the others. "Listen, I hear something in the bushes. It could be one of those things. We better keep our spears at the ready and hurry along. Try to be quiet. They will hear us."

The last man of the six travelers who trailed at the back of the group sighed and moved along at his own sluggish pace. He was hungry and tired and did not hear the others' warning. It was too late when he did hear something at his back but could not yell out to the others before he was pulled apart and swallowed by two hungry Catlings.

The men ahead of him heard a noise and turned around to see what it was. They put their spears in front of them and backed into a circle protecting one another's backs. There was nothing there now but they noticed a trail of blood behind them and one of their men was missing.

The leader of this group whispered, "We need to back away as quickly as we can and get into Sovorotskina for protection. The Catlings cannot go into the village. Maybe we can figure out a way to cross over the barrier to safety."

One anxious man said, "How do we do that? If the Catlings can't get through, what makes you think that we can? We did find a way to cross through the border near Votovia into the UT."

"The border is not as protected there as in Sovorotskina. We need to call for help. Someone will hear us."

High up in the trees the Sprites were watching and listening to the men discuss this. The Sprites had their own discussions amongst themselves whether these men were worth the effort to save.

"What do you think we should do?" one Sprite asked another.

"Well, they look like they are up to no good."

"I agree," another responded.

"They are coming to Sovorotskina to kill someone with the spears they have. We can't let them through the barriers of the borders. I think we should summon Spindle. He will know what to do."

"Yes, Spindle will know what to do," another Sprite agreed.

"Well, we better hurry up before they all get eaten by the Catlings. The Cats are mean enough when they are not hungry. They have been hiding out from the beams as we have and are now starving."

Spindle heard the message from his fellow Sprites and flew to the tree where these Sprites were now pointing down to the five men in a circle with spears.

Spindle called down to the men, "What are you doing here? Who are you?"

"Please help us. One of our men was already devoured by these cat-like creatures. We will explain as soon as you help us get out of here."

"Oh, you mean the Catlings? They don't mean you any harm. I think they may have had their fill for now. Tell me why you are here?"

The leader of the men responded in an anxious manner, "I...we...need to speak to King Gateskin. We have a message for him from King Kaposkaran of Parotovina."

"I will help you. I promise you though that I will kill you myself if you threaten anyone in Sovorotskina, especially our King."

"Of course, we understand. Now hu..hurry they are coming back," the man said in a shaky voice.

Before the men could say another word, Spindle had picked them up two at a time with the help of his fellow Sprites, brought them through the border, and set them down on the ground. He flew above them and waited for an explanation of what they would say to the King.

"What did you want to tell our King?"

"Well, we need to see him and only him."

"I am his Head Guard and I can relay the message for you. I cannot let you go near him or the village itself. You will stay here until I return."

"But we could be in danger again."

"No, you will not be in danger. You will stay here tied to this tree until I return. If you try to escape, I will send one or all of our dragons to get you."

"All of your dragons? How many dragons do you have?"

Spindle tied the men to the tree with fibers that he had attached to his belt and stepped back. "There, that should hold all of you. Don't forget, if you try to escape, I will send the dragons to keep you in line."

"Yes, we understand!" the leader stated as he exchanged anxious looks with his men.

Spindle flew to the dragons' lair first and instructed one of them to watch over the men until he could return with King Gateskin.

"Callum or Evander, can you please keep an eye on the five men I tied to the tree near the border? I found them trying to get through to see the King."

"Certainly, little man. It would be our pleasure, Evander, right?"

"Sure. We will find them and make sure they do not move a muscle," Evander chuckled.

Madrigal looked up at Spindle. "Do you need me to assist?"

"No, Madrigal. Take care of Izara. I think Callum and Evander can handle things. Thank you though."

"Well, I am here if you need me," Madrigal added.

"How is Izara doing?" Spindle asked.

"She is doing quite well and sleeping on and off. I think the Queen gave her some sleeping pill or spell to ward off the pain until she heals."

"I think you are right about that. Well, take care of her. I will return shortly."

Spindle messaged the King and was met by Gateskin halfway there.

"What's going on, Spindle? More trouble with the Catlings?"

"Sort of, but this involves King Parotovina's men coming to see you to deliver a message from him."

"Let's go see them and find out what they need to tell me. It can't be anything good."

"I agree, King."

On their way back to the men, Spindle explained what happened to the unfortunate man who was eaten by the Catlings.

Gateskin shook his head in disbelief that King Kaposkaran would continue to send men to their deaths through the UT just to get to him.

CHAPTER THIRTY-FIVE

Callum and Evander were flying around the startled men who looked up at them with frightened expressions as the dragons caused a wind to whip at the men.

"I like this, Callum. This can be fun to do."

"I was afraid of that. We were not told to torment them in any way, just to watch over them so they wouldn't escape.

"I know, but that would be boring. I am all for some fun and this is fun to do. Look at the men's eyes! It looks like they will pop right out of their heads any time now. Can you imagine if I blew smoke at them?" Evander stated with a snicker.

"You will do no such thing, Evander. Behave yourself."

Just as Evander was preparing to cause more chaos with the frightened men, Spindle and King Gateskin arrived.

"King Gateskin, how nice to see you again," Evander said, as he bowed to the King.

"Good to see you too, Evander. Did I hear that you were causing some havoc here for these men?"

"Oh, no, well, not too much, King. I was just having a little fun with them. I think they are here to cause trouble," Evander confessed.

King Gateskin gave Evander a stern look and focused thereafter on the shivering men.

"Who do we have here?"

The leader of the men raised his hand as far as he could from under the ropes and said, "I am their leader, King Gateskin. We are most grateful to your Head Guard Spindle for rescuing us from those Catlings. Those vile creatures ate one of my men and would have eaten all of us soon if Spindle hadn't come."

"Who sent you here?"

"King Kaposkaran sent us to talk to you about the dragons."

"What does he want to know about my dragons?"

"He said that you have two and he wants to find out how he can get one for himself." The other four men whispered to him, "That's not what he wanted us to do."

"Oh, he does, does he? You can tell him that they are not for sale and there is no way he can ever have one," Gateskin emphasized.

"I see. But he will kill us all if we return without one."

"Do you really think that you can wrestle a dragon and bring it back with you?"

"Well, not really. If you command one to go with us, maybe that would work. We fear for our lives and that of our families if we don't do this."

"What do you think that your King will do with a dragon?"

"I don't know, King Gateskin. I think he wants to protect the village."

"Do you really believe that?"

"Well, I would like to believe that. I know otherwise. What are we going to do? We can't return. If we don't return our families will be killed. Can you help us?"

King Gateskin looked at the other four men who were shaking their heads in disagreement.

"What is wrong? Don't you four agree with your leader?"

"No, we don't, King Gateskin. Only part of what our leader told you is the truth," one man stated.

"What part is that?"

"The part that the King would kill us and our families if we do not return."

"Did your King send you here to take one of my dragons away with you to Parotovina?"

"No, absolutely not, King Gateskin. What he told us to do was to disrupt your plans to train them and cause trouble for you so that you would not be successful."

"Hmm, I see. That is more like it." Turning to the leader, Gateskin said, "So you lied to me."

"Well, not really. It would be a feather in our caps or maybe just mine if I could do such a thing as to bring a dragon back to him."

"I bet it would," Gateskin guffawed as the dragons laughed along with him at such a preposterous idea.

Evander huffed and puffed out a ring of smoke that encircled the terrified men.

"There is no need for that, Evander. I think they got the picture already," King Gateskin answered with a wave of his hand that blew the smoke away. This smoke could render the men helpless and into a deep sleep if they breathed it in too long.

Callum poked Evander in the head with his wing.

"Hey, what was that for?" Evander asked in surprise.

"You know what it was for – a warning. Behave yourself," Callum said with a stern look that could freeze anyone in their tracks.

Evander just smirked at Callum and bowed his head as he sighed. "Okay, I guess."

King Gateskin asked Spindle to untie the men and bring them to his home. He wanted to discuss this more with them.

"Yes, King, right away. Let's go, men."

"Do you need our assistance, King Gateskin?" Evander asked with a wistful expression.

"No, you can return to your lair. You will be receiving dinner a little later. You will also get an extra treat for your help today before that though."

"That sounds grand, King. I can't wait," Evander said with a grin.

Callum sighed and pushed his fellow dragon along as they flew back to their lair.

Spindle followed behind the King with the four men still tied together within his grasp. They squirmed and settled down once he held them tighter as he flew above them.

When they arrived back at the King's home, Spindle released the men and instructed them to sit down until the King was ready to speak with them.

Queen Solinara went out to the kitchen and prepared some refreshments for the men but did not speak with them. She had gotten the message from Gateskin to ignore them for they should not be treated like honored guests. They would be fed and sent on their way after being reprimanded by the King.

The men were tired and hungry and welcomed the food even if no one looked at or spoke to them until they were finished eating.

Gateskin focused on the men and asked, "Did you have enough to eat?"

"Yes, we are thankful for your hospitality, King and Queen. We don't deserve your kindness. I am sorry for lying to you before."

"We treat everyone with kindness, respect, and hospitality even if they do not respond as such to us," King retorted.

"We were frightened, King, and did not know what to do. Our lives were in jeopardy no matter what we did," the leader stated.

"I can see that. I know how dangerous your king can be to his people. I want to help you though. You must return and tell the King that you were successful in thwarting my efforts to train the dragons."

"Will we be truthful? He will know if we are not."

"Yes, he will believe you because I will put a spell on you to prevent him from discovering that you are lying."

"You can do that, King Gateskin?"

"Yes, I can do that easily enough."

"Okay. What do we have to do?" the Parotovinan guard asked.

"Just relax and breathe deeply. I will put you under a spell and you won't remember any of what I am doing. You will remember being attacked by the Catlings and being rescued by the Sprites but that is all."

"How will we convince the King that we know that you have been unsuccessful in your training?"

"You will tell him that the dragons were disrespectful and did not listen to me as you watched them in action. You will also say that you escaped thereafter.

"He will not believe that, King. I am fearful that he will see through this lie."

"He will not see it as a lie. He will believe it for you will believe it too. That is the secret to this spell. It is a spell that will convince you and him that it is the truth. I can't call it a truth spell. It is really an Exaggeration of the Truth Spell. This will be the first time that I have created something like this."

The men nodded and closed their eyes as the King prepared to put them under this new spell. Gateskin crossed his fingers that it would work as he chanted the spell and spread it over the men and deposited them safely out of the UT.

When the men woke up, they found themselves on the outskirts of Sovorotskina. They traveled as quickly as they could through the different villages, not meeting the eyes of any of the inhabitants until they arrived back in Parotovina.

Spindle watched the men leave the border of Sovorotskina, and kept in touch with his fellow Sprites who reported as the men passed each village and were finally back in Parotovina.

The men went directly to the King's palace to report their mission was a success except for the loss of one of their men.

CHAPTER THIRTY-SIX

King Kaposkaran got word that his guards were back from their mission. He told his palace guards to escort them into his conference room right away.

The five guards stood at attention until they were requested to answer the King's questions.

"What happened in Sovorotskina?"

The leader of the guards answered and explained what had happened to them in the UT and how the Catlings ate one of the men.

"How did you escape these creatures?"

The guard responded by saying, "We were rescued by the Sprites. The Head Guard, Spindle, took us out of the UT to safety and we escaped and came back home."

"Did you see the dragons?"

"Yes, we did," another guard answered.

"And what happened?"

"We saw them in action being disrespectful to King Gateskin. They wouldn't listen to him."

"Ahh, I see. So, it looks as if he is not doing well with them."

"Yes, King," the guard assented.

"Do you think you could return there and bring one of those dragons back here?"

The five men exchanged looks. "I don't know, King Kaposkaran. I don't think we can do that. They are dangerous and will attack us if we try to do that," one guard answered after conferring with the others.

"Well, I want one of those dragons. I will send more men to assist you. You will go back to Sovorotskina and bring one to me or…"

The men shivered at the lack of words that the King left unsaid. They knew what he meant.

"How will we do that, King? We are only defenseless men. They will kill us all."

"Maybe not. I have a plan. Wait here."

The King disappeared and returned with Queen Beregina. The King and Queen whispered between them and turned to the men who did not know what to expect.

"My queen has come up with a new spell that can be used to capture one of the dragons. All you have to do is give the dragon a taste of this liquid. They will become docile and do whatever you ask of them."

The men's faces expressed their bewilderment at this. "How can we do that? We can't get close enough to them to administer this."

"You will put the liquid on some meat. They will eat anything that they can and will never know what had hit them."

"Don't you want only one dragon, King? You said them."

"Well, if it works on one; it could work on both. Besides, if you feed one dragon, the other will want some too. This way you can keep the second dragon from attacking you before it realizes what you did."

"Can we go home to our families and rest a bit? We are tired from our long journey."

"Yes, go home and prepare your supplies for another trip. I will gather several more men to go with you. You will also need a cart large enough to transport the dragons back here. Come back tonight at 8:00. That should be enough time to rest and prepare yourselves for another trip."

"Yes, King," the men answered and left the palace, mumbling to each other.

"What about the Catlings? We will get eaten by them for sure. How are we going to stay away from them?" one guard asked.

"I don't know," the leader stated with a shake of his head. "I don't know."

The King and Queen watched the men leave and discussed how this would work.

"Are you sure that the dragons will eat this? Will they suspect that it is tainted?"

"No, Kaposkaran. I don't think they will. They are ravenous creatures and will eat anything that will fit into their mouths. By the time the potion takes effect, it will make them complacent and more receptive to being taken. They will never know what happened to them."

"I like that, Beregina. You have outdone yourself, dear."

"Thank you, Kaposkaran. I think I did. Was there any doubt about that?"

"No, I guess there wasn't. I forgot how powerful you could be since the Moss Spell."

"Well, I need to go back and do some more testing on this spell before the guards leave to ensure that it is strong enough for a powerful creature like a dragon. I will need to add more spells to it to reinforce the strength."

"That sounds like a sensible thing to do, Beregina. I have things to do also. I need to get more men and a large cart for transportation. We will know in a few days' time whether we are successful in stealing a dragon or two. I would love to see King Gateskin's face when he discovers them missing," King Kaposkaran laughed out loud as he called out to his palace guards to bring several more guards to him.

***

Back on Sovorotskina, King Gateskin did not like the feel in the air coming from down south. He was not worried that the guards would remember what he told them about the spell. He was more concerned about what King Kaposkaran would do next. The Parotovinan King would not be happy with his plan being unsuccessful.

Gateskin went to discuss this with Spindle and Mitteran, his Head Guards. He would put them on alert at the borders to keep watch for any more guards coming their way. He wanted to be prepared for whatever plan the evil king was in the process of devising.

CHAPTER THIRTY-SEVEN

The Sprites in the outskirts of Parotovina watched and listened to what was going on in the village of Parotovina. They saw several guards gathered at the entrance of the palace suited up for travel. These men were in the process of building an enormous cart to transport something quite large.

"What do you think King Kaposkaran is working on now? It could be trouble for King Gateskin. Maybe we should start singing our song to slow them down again. We know that if they are heading to Sovorotskina, they will bring nothing but trouble," several Sprites discussed this among themselves.

"Yes, I agree," another Sprite stated with a grin. "I always enjoy singing and causing havoc for King Kaposkaran."

The Sprites, who were many, gathered high in the treetops and began their song as soon as the group of guards began to march through the forest. The Sprites had spread word that they would sing as one to deter the journey of the guards before they arrived at their destination of Sovorotskina.

From the Land of Darkness

To the Land of Light

We never let our enemies out of our sight.

As we travel high and travel low,

We always stay safe wherever we go.

May Faith & Love be with us each day.

May Magic & Mystery conjure up the words we need to say.

May Peace & Harmony guide us on our way.

May Myths & Legends help us to stay strong, we pray.

Spindle received the message from the Sprites and joined in singing their treasured song that had been sung for many a year. He smiled to himself as he traveled along to see the King to share what was coming their way once again.

Mitteran listened and chuckled when he heard Spindle singing along with the echoes of fellow Sprites' voices throughout the land. He turned to Spindle and called out, "I will keep watch. You keep singing. I didn't know how talented you were as a singer or the other Sprites for that matter."

Spindle nodded in thanks and waved as he flew back to see the King.

Serena heard Spindle's beautiful voice as she was feeding the wolves along with her mother and siblings. She looked up with eyes full of love and sighed, "Why are you singing, Spindle?"

"My fellow Sprites are warning me about what is coming this way. I need to see your father right away."

"You have a lovely voice, Spindle. You should sing more often," Serena said as her cheeks grew pinker than usual.

"Thank you, Serena. I appreciate that. My family doesn't always agree with that."

Serena giggled and pointed the way to her father who was in the Queen's workshop. She called out to Spindle before he got too far, "What is that? A sword?"

Turing back to Serena, the Sprite responded, "Yes, do you like it? Alaric, the blacksmith made it for me."

"It is quite beautiful with the jewels on the handle. Are you going to use it?" Serena asked feeling a little apprehensive about this.

"Well, only in dire emergencies, Serena. Sorry, but I need to see the King. Talk to you later."

"Hmm. Okay, stay safe, Spindle."

He nodded and flew to the King's home.

The King looked up as he heard the door open and saw Spindle flying there. The dragon ladies were there with him and listened to the exchange.

"Something is happening, Spindle?"

"Yes, King. There are several guards coming this way again from Parotovina. The Sprites told me that they are dragging a cart this time."

"A cart?"

"Yes, a large one that would transport something huge."

"Hmm, I see. I wonder what they think they are going to transport from here?"

"I wonder," Spindle guffawed.

"Well, we will see about that, won't we. Let's go visit the dragons to warn them."

Aharona and Navaeha joined in, "We will follow you and assist with our dragons, King."

"I'm right with you, King. This should be interesting," Spindle chirped in.

"Before we get there, take the new dragons aside and keep them occupied while I speak with Callum and Evander. They are more experienced dealing with these men. I don't want anyone injured or killed. We will find a way to fix this situation without harm."

"Whatever you say, King." Spindle flew ahead to keep Madrigal and Izara busy while the King conversed with the other two dragons.

Callum and Evander were nodding off once again on one of their several daily naps when King Gateskin called out to them to come out of the lair.

"Yes, King. What is it? This sounds ominous," Callum retorted.

"It is. We need to move away from here a little. I don't want the other two dragons to hear this. They have much to learn about how to handle situations like this."

Evander flew along with Callum behind the King to a place far enough away from the lair to hear what the King had to say. They looked to their mistresses who nodded for them to listen to the King.

"Is there trouble brewing again, King?" Callum asked as he tucked in his wings to listen.

"I'm afraid there is, Callum," King Gateskin said as he explained what Spindle had said about the travelers.

"What would you like us to do, King?" Evander asked, eagerness in his deep voice.

"No, I don't want anyone harmed in this confrontation. I will speak with the men when they get here."

"That is, if they arrive without being slaughtered by the Catlings. I think they are procreating more lately to reinforce their dwindling numbers," Callum announced.

"Yes, I agree. You will keep watch over the borders. When you hear them coming, fly over the UT and keep the Catlings at bay so that the men can pass through the borders when I give you the word," Gateskin responded with a sigh.

Callum and Evander nodded and flew up into the UT on alert.

Spindle was visiting with the other two dragons and asking them all kinds of questions to keep them busy.

"So, what is going on, Spindle?" Madrigal asked as he stood up and spread out his wings.

"Something is going on," Izara said as she licked her injured wing, which was getting better day by day, out of habit more than to lessen the pain which was now gone, thanks to the Queen.

"I should have known better than to fool you wise creatures. You do have a sixth sense like I do. We may be two different creatures but underneath we are more alike than you think," Spindle said with a grin.

"I guess, but certainly a lot larger, Spindle," Madrigal snickered.

Izara giggled and spread her wings in agreement before asking, "Are you going to tell us what is going on?"

Spindle sighed and explained.

"I see. The King needs our help. We will do whatever he needs us to do to keep him and all of you safe here in Sovorotskina, our new home," Madrigal exclaimed.

"Do you agree, Izara?" Spindle probed, watching the female dragon as she mused over what her mate had said.

"Well, I guess I have to agree with Madrigal. We need to keep things safe here since we are living alongside all of you."

"Nicely said, Izara!" Madrigal grinned at her with a twinkle in his eye.

"I could change my mind again later, Madrigal. Don't get too cozy with staying here yet."

Madrigal nodded and winked at Spindle who smiled back at him.

"Let me see what the King wants you to do. Wait here," Spindle stated as he flew to find the King.

The King was heading back to see him and the new dragons. "You told them, Spindle?"

"Yes, I'm afraid so, King. They surmised that something was going on."

"Hmm, I guessed as much."

"Well, they both agreed to help you in any way they could. What would you like to do, King?"

"Good to hear, Spindle. I was hoping they would be willing to assist."

"What really surprised me was that Izara is more in tune with staying here than before. It could have something to do with the injury she sustained and the healing by the Queen."

"The Queen will be pleased to hear that. Now this is what we will do," Gateskin began.

"That is certainly good news, King," Aharona admitted as Navaeha nodded.

"We can fly on our dragons' backs and watch over the borders with them, King." Navaeha added.

"Madrigal and Izara can follow you and keep eyes on the trees," Gateskin instructed.

"We are at your service, King," Madrigal and Izara responded and flew in behind the other two dragons.

"Please be careful. I don't trust those Catlings to try and attack you from the trees. They can climb quite far. The Sprites keep them away from their young by stinging them with a spell of their own."

"We will be, King. They are clever little critters, aren't they?" Aharona chuckled.

"You have no idea how clever these Sprites can be, ladies," Gateskin announced.

CHAPTER THIRTY-EIGHT

Queen Solinara finished the feeding of the wolves with her children's help and moved the children indoors. She had received a message from Gateskin that there was trouble heading their way once again.

"What is going on now, Mother?" Serena asked as they were once again inside their home.

"I know I can't hide anything from you three, Serena," Solinara stated as she began to explain what was transpiring as they sat there.

"Does Father need our help?" Simon asked, eager to assist.

"No, he has Spindle and four dragons and their mistresses helping him. I think that is more than enough."

"What if something happened to Spindle?" Serena's voice quivered in concern.

"Your father would never let anything happen to Spindle or anyone else in our village. No need to worry, Serena. I know how you feel about this Sprite."

"I...I can't help worrying. I worry about everyone here."

"Yes, I know you do, sweetie. I do too. Now let's prepare something special for your father. He will need something substantial for dinner tonight. It could be a long night for all of them."

The children nodded glumly and began to follow their mother's directions.

Serena tried to listen in to her father's plans with Spindle. She knew her mother was right about everything and how Father would protect her favorite Sprite, but she couldn't help being concerned just the same. She had to do something.

Gateskin could feel his oldest daughter's mind trying to connect with him. He couldn't believe how strong she was becoming. He resisted and put a strong Block Spell over his mind to keep her out. He didn't want her to know just how dangerous this mission was for all of them.

In Parotovina the King paced back and forth mumbling to himself. "This better work or I don't know what I will do. I know how strong Beregina's spells can be and also how dangerous. I only hope that it doesn't kill the dragons. I would rather have one alive. On the other hand, the head of the dragon would look quite impressive over my fireplace in this conference room." The King called his men to bring him something to eat as he continued to muse some more about all this.

Queen Beregina continued to work on some more potions in case the one she gave to the guards for the dragons wasn't successful. What she now discovered was something shocking.

She used a common bug she had found on the ground to experiment on. When she gave the bug a drop of the potion that was for the dragons, it grew in size but became distorted before it died. It did not fall asleep at all.

Adding another ingredient to the potion she tried again with another unsuspecting bug that happened to wander into her workshop. This time the bug fell asleep but continued to grow and become more grotesque during slumber.

She kept trying by adding another ingredient and also by putting a spell on the next bug so it wouldn't change in size. The bug did not grow and only became even more ugly than the others. This appeared to be some kind of glitch. She couldn't figure out what that could be.

The Queen destroyed all the sleeping bugs and began again with a new potion. Now she was worried that she had been too hasty in giving the guards the other potion. It had worked when she first tried it. What could have happened? Maybe it will work better on the dragons than it did on the insects. She could only hope. Should she tell the King?

Beregina went for a walk in the palace garden to clear her mind before doing anything else. She could not share any of this failure with her husband. He would never trust her again. He was still peeved about the Moss Spell and how much time and energy it cost him to clean it up. There were still occasionally some growing that she had to take care of since he refused to do it any longer.

***

The voices of the Sprites rang through the forest of the UT as they tried to intimidate the guards from going any further. The men had tried to keep the sound out of their ears and had given up trying. They trudged along at a slower pace now because of the Sprites' efforts.

Just ahead the Catlings patrolled looking for something to eat. They stayed away from the borders since they could not penetrate the barriers set there by Sovorotskina. They stayed in the middle of the deep forest to search.

There were no smaller creatures around anymore. The Catlings had decimated them long ago. If there were any that survived, they may not be able to procreate if they did not have any females left.

Catlings were not only fierce but also intelligent creatures who always kept their females safe in the burrows with the young. The males were the hunters unlike some animals of the animal kingdom.

The Catlings felt a wind pick up above them as they saw four large dragons flying over their land. They hunkered down to stay out of sight of these creatures. They knew that they could not defend themselves against these dragons especially if they blew fire at them. They waited until the dragons passed over them before moving on.

The sound of many footsteps could be heard making the Catlings' ears perk up. Also, they could smell the bodies of humans coming their way. They weren't sure what the other noise was that sounded like a large object being rolled along. They waited in the bushes to see what it was and if it could be dangerous to them.

The men slowed down and listened. The leader of the guards queried, "Did you hear that?"

"What? I didn't hear anything," another said.

"No, I didn't either," more men replied.

"Well, keep your eyes and ears open for any of those vicious Catlings. We know what they can do," the leader urged.

Before the men could move much farther, the Catlings were in front of them. The leader of the guards pulled out the potion and put a few drops on some pieces of meat and threw it away from them to steer the animals in another direction so they could escape. The Catlings sniffed the meat and gulped it down.

The men stepped close together to watch what would happen to the Catlings. They didn't have to wait long. The animals began to grow and change into something more hideous than they already were.

"What happened? They were supposed to fall asleep," one frightened man exclaimed as he backed further away trying to find a way to escape.

"I don't know. What are we going to do now? They are even bigger than before."

"Wait a minute. Look at them! They are acting strange and walking around in circles. Maybe they will fall asleep soon."

The Catlings began to turn on one another and attack their own kind instead of going after the men. There was blood and guts flying around as the men moved away as quickly as they could. They couldn't keep their eyes off of these changed creatures and what they were doing to each other.

The Sprites were also witnessing this horror and covered their children's eyes and ears to the massacre. They sent an alert to Spindle about what was happening. Their singing had ceased.

The sounds of the attack were also heard by the four dragons and the mistresses who were flying nearby. They swooped down closer to see what was happening.

"What is going on? Look at the Catlings! They are growing and attacking each other. What could have caused that?" Aharona quizzed.

"I don't know. Look over there, the men are running away. They don't appear to be harmed. Did they do something to the Catlings?" Navaeha asked.

"That's a good question. Let's alert the King to open up the border for the men and we will find out," Aharona replied.

CHAPTER THIRTY-NINE

Callum and Evander wanted to dip down to taste some of the fresh Catling meat but their mistresses forbade it.

"Listen, you two. Something is wrong here. We don't want you anywhere near the Catlings or whatever they have turned into. They could be poisoned with something and transfer that to you. We don't want anything like that to happen to either of you rascals even if you are both more problematic than we can handle at times," Aharona cried out in a strong voice.

"Do you understand?" Navaeha questioned her charge.

"Yes, Mistress. We do understand. But all this carnage has made our stomachs ache with hunger. Isn't it almost dinnertime anyway?" Evander sighed.

Callum nodded to his mistress and did his best to look contrite.

"Don't worry about that. Let's go see the King and find out what these men can tell us," Aharona stated in a firm voice.

"Do you need us to assist too?" Madrigal asked.

"No, I think Callum and Evander can handle this," Gateskin responded. "But thank you for offering. You did enough already."

Spindle and King Gateskin arrived at the border at the same time to talk to the frazzled men and the hungry dragons.

Aharona explained what she witnessed along with her sister and the dragons. "We don't know what happened to cause these creatures to change like that, King."

"Hmm, I see. Let's hear what the guards from Parotovina have to say about all this." Turning to the men, King Gateskin asked, "Well, what do you have to say for yourselves?"

The leader stepped forward and, in a stammer, tried to explain, "I…we…tried to protect ourselves."

"How did you protect yourselves? Did you do this to the Catlings?"

The guard looked at his men and shrugged his shoulders. "We only used a potion that King Kaposkaran gave us created by Queen Beregina."

"Now I understand. So, you were coming here to try that on me?"

"Oh, no, King Gateskin. We would never do that!" one man exclaimed in horror.

"We only wanted to steal one or both of your dragons," another man stated before he could stop himself.

"Idiot!" the leader of the guards yelled. "Why did you tell him that?"

"Now it all makes sense. Let me see if I truly understand what your plan was. You would come here with this outrageous cart, use the potion on my dragons and take them back with you to Parotovina to your king. Is that correct?"

"Well…um…maybe," the guard responded in reluctance.

"How were you planning on getting my dragons into your cart if they were to change like that?"

"Well, they were supposed to go to sleep with the potion, not do this," the leader replied.

"How do you explain what happened?"

"We don't know. We don't understand how this could have happened. It wasn't supposed to do that to the Catlings."

"What do you think I should do with you now?" King Gateskin asked.

"We…we…have to return. You can't kill us or the King will murder our families. We must return even if we are unsuccessful."

"I see. Well, maybe I can help you. I will have the dragons burn up the carcasses of the Catlings and put them on your cart. You can carry them back with you and explain what happened with the potion."

"I…I don't think the King will like that," the guard stated in a quiver.

"Well, whether he likes it or not, that is what you will do. You cannot now or ever take one of my dragons back to him. Do you understand me?" King Gateskin raised his voice and gave them a steely-eyed stare that froze them in place.

"Yes, yes, sir. We understand. We need to leave right away. Thank you," the guard said, refusing to meet the King's eyes.

"Good. Now let's get some carcasses for you to transport. I don't want to see you back here again. Do you understand?"

"Yes, King Gateskin," the fearful men recited in unison.

The two dragons dipped down, thoroughly burned the carcasses, and put them onto the cart. They did not dare lick their claws for their mistresses were keeping watch over them and instructed them to clean off their claws in the hot water that the King brought out of thin air and offered to them.

The surviving Catlings had disappeared back to their burrows having escaped by not eating any of the tainted meat.

The King watched the men leave until they were beyond his borders and into Votovia. He messaged King Cavelan of Votovia to keep an eye on these men and did the same to the other rulers along the way in warning about the carnage that they would see and most likely smell as it passed through their lands.

He assured them that these men would not pose any danger to their villages or peoples. He did add that it was best to keep their animals far away from the cart because of the tainted meat that could harm them if eaten.

They all replied that they would keep him informed as the men passed through their lands and finally arrived at the border of Parotovina.

When King Kaposkaran saw the men passing through the Guard House, he hurried out to meet them. He saw the cart without any dragons. Instead, his nose was assaulted by a hideous smell of burned flesh.

Queen Beregina was looking out her window when she noticed this cart absent of dragons but with something else burned beyond recognition. She hid in her workshop and did not come out even when her husband called out to her.

CHAPTER FORTY

King Cavelan of Votovia messaged King Gateskin right after seeing the men and the cart pass through his village.

"What's going on, my friend?" he queried.

Gateskin answered quickly from his conference room after opening the Channel Spell.

He explained to Cavelan what had transpired or at least what he thought had happened to the Catlings.

"Will Kaposkaran ever stop trying to interfere in everything that you try to do?"

"Evidently not. He enjoys doing this. He is not happy with what he has in his own kingdom and only covets what I or others have."

"How are your new dragons doing?"

"Very well, Cavelan. Surprisingly well. I only have a few more days to meet the criteria of King Marcellus in order to keep them. His daughters will be returning to inform him of our success soon."

"Wonderful news, Gateskin. I am happy to hear that. What else do they need to do?"

"I need to fly on their backs one at a time and have them perform some more tasks without the dragon ladies around. They need to know that they will not have to obey the ladies, just me."

"I hope it all works out for you, Gateskin. Maybe there is hope for me too to have one someday."

"That I can't say for sure, Cavelan. Don't give up hope. I can always be there to guide you if that day comes."

"I would appreciate your help. I don't want to get my hopes up just yet. Time will tell. I'll let you go. I'm sure you need to do many other things today before the day ends. Talk to you soon."

"I do, my friend, and we will talk again soon."

Gateskin turned to Spindle who was flitting around over his head waiting for more orders.

"Don't fret, Spindle. We will get to look over the UT for any more issues with the Catlings soon. Please check with your fellow Sprites to see if it is all quiet there now. I will have the dragons and you fly over for a sweep of the area. I don't want to see any sick Catlings straying too close to the borders."

"Yes, King." Spindle flew away to message the Sprites in the UT.

The Sprites were cleaning up the area of the burnt offerings when they received a message from Spindle.

"All is quiet here, Spindle," one Sprite announced. "We are cleaning up the area. It stinks something awful. We used a few spells of our own to clear it out. It is still lingering a little, probably stuck in our noses, I guess," the Sprite sighed.

"I can help if you need me," Spindle retorted. "The King needs you to keep alert for any other problems."

"No, I think we are good here, Spindle, but thank you. We will definitely keep alert to anything out of the ordinary. Please tell the King we are his eyes and ears at all times."

One Sprite looked up at Spindle and asked, "What is that at your belt?"

"It's a sword that was made by Alaric, the blacksmith. Do you like it?" Spindle said with pride.

"I certainly do," the Sprite responded with a wide grin. "It is beautiful and it has jewels on it. Do you plan on using it?"

"Not unless I absolutely need to."

"That's good. I wish I had one of those," the Sprite sighed. "You are one very lucky Sprite,"

"Yes, I know. Thank you," Spindle responded with a smile, feeling a great respect and kinship with his fellow Sprites. The sword never left his side after that.

Spindle flew over to find Mitteran and inform him about the Catlings and the guards.

"I did smell something nauseating and didn't know what it was. I was at the other end of the border. It all appears quiet there with no sign of the Catlings."

"Thanks, Mitteran. The King says we need to keep our eyes and ears alert. The Catlings may come out sooner or later out of curiosity. I'm sure for now they are a little anxious about what transpired."

"Yes, I would be too, Spindle. Is there anything else you or the King need, my friend? Is that new on your belt?"

"Yes, it's a sword made by Alaric."

"That is most impressive. You must have done something special to warrant a gift like that," Mitteran stated with a grin.

"Well, he gave it to me for protecting the villagers. I am most grateful."

"I would be too if he made me one. It looks good on you, Spindle."

"Thanks, Mitteran. There isn't anything else for you to do. Just keep patrolling the borders on this end and let me know if you see anything suspicious with the Catlings or anything else."

"Will do. I will report to King Gateskin when I break for dinner."

"Good idea. Thanks again."

Spindle flew around the village looking here and there and spread word to the people not to be afraid. Everything was safe for them to continue to farm and take care of their animals.

He did tell one of the men, "Please stay away from the borders of the UT just in case one of the Catlings gets too brazen. We don't expect them to break through the border. I don't want one of the children to get curious about them and venture too close."

"We already gave them the word about that. I am keeping my children busy picking vegetables from the garden and feeding the animals. They are curious though about the dragons and want to visit them. Will we be able to see the dragons soon?"

"I will check with the King about that. They are still in training. I'm sure there will be a time when King Gateskin will introduce them to the village."

"I will tell my children that. If they promise to be on their best behavior, they will see the dragons soon."

"Yes, that could work, sir," Spindle responded with a chuckle. "Please spread word to the others about keeping a distance from the borders."

"Certainly, I can do that, Spindle. Good day."

"Good day to you too."

As Spindle flew over the village others who were out in the gardens looked up and waved at him. He responded by doing a dip and a flip to the delight of the children. He always enjoyed entertaining them every chance he could get.

He smiled to himself and thought. "Maybe one day I will have children of my own. I wonder how that could ever be if I am just a stick and my love is human," he sighed.

There was a noise coming from the dragons' lair as Spindle flew over. He dropped down and looked inside. He wasn't expecting to see this.

CHAPTER FORTY-ONE

The four dragons looked up when they spotted Spindle flying around inside their lair.

"What's going on here?" Spindle asked.

"Nothing too serious, Sprite. We were just having a wrestling match. I am tired of being the smallest dragon," Izara stated with a grunt.

"I tried to tell her, Spindle, that she is not the smallest dragon ever. There are plenty that are smaller," Madrigal said.

"Hmm, I see. What about you, Evander? Are you being a bully toward Izara?"

"Not at all, Spindle. I was trying to convince her that she did not have to wrestle me to win my respect. I know that she is strong for her size."

"Are you getting hungry by any chance?" Spindle enquired.

"Well, as a matter of fact, we are, and bored too. We need to do something other than sitting around here," Izara complained.

"I will see to your dinner. Try to behave yourselves and stay out of trouble until I return," Spindle stressed as he turned and flew away.

"I hope he doesn't report our mischief to the King," Madrigal stated with a frown at his mate.

"Don't worry. Spindle is our friend. He will honor our privacy," Izara stated with a smirk.

"You better hope so," Madrigal warned. "Did you notice the sword Spindle has in his scabbard?"

"No, I didn't. Why would he have a sword? Was he planning on using it on us? Never mind that. I am not afraid of King Gateskin. In fact, I am not afraid of anyone or anything," Izara continued.

"Maybe you better be, Izara, if you want to get along and live here. Spindle may have to use the sword on you sometime if you don't behave better. At least show some respect to King Gateskin and Queen Solinara and their family," Madrigal insisted.

"I show them respect, don't I?"

"Hmm, I don't know about that. You have been giving the King trouble and being obstinate since we arrived. What is wrong, Izara? Is there something that I can do to help you adjust?"

"I...I...oh, never mind. Just leave me alone, Madrigal!" Izara flew to another part of their lair past the other two dragons who were sleeping or trying to sleep in spite of all the noise that Izara was making with her complaining.

Madrigal sighed and raised his wings and flew out of the lair to wait outside for Spindle to return with their food.

Back at the Queen's workshop, Spindle was speaking with her about the restless and hungry dragons. "What can we do about the dragons, Queen?"

"Don't worry too much, Spindle. Once they are fed, they will be more amenable to our ways here."

"I guess you are right, Queen Solinara. You are wise and always right."

"Haha, tell that to the King!" Queen giggled and continued packing extra food to bring to the dragons. She added a little extra something to Izara's food that would help make her feel calmer and more agreeable when spoken to. She hoped this would work. They would find out soon enough.

"I will bring these over to them now. If you want to come along and see how they react after they finish eating, please do."

"I plan to stay close by, Queen, in case they give you any trouble."

"I don't expect that to happen, Spindle. Maybe I should give you some of my special food to calm you down too."

"Oh, sorry. I didn't mean to come across as anxious. I am fine and calm, my queen."

"That's good, Spindle. I know you are especially good under pressure. I have seen your courage and tenacity to complete each task you are given. The King and I are very proud of you."

"Oh, my, I am humbled, Queen. I don't know what to say."

"No need to say anymore, Spindle. Come with me. Let's take care of those hungry dragons."

"Yes, Queen." Spindle bowed his head and blushed a green tint to his wooden face.

The dragons were awake and waiting as patiently as they could for their dinner. They had been rewarded with a tasty creature each for helping the King in the UT with the Catlings earlier. That didn't stop them from being hungry again.

Madrigal was out front and spotted the Queen and Spindle flying their way with large tubs full of food. Madrigal flew up to meet them. "Can I assist you, Queen?"

"No need, Madrigal, but thank you just the same. I will bring the tubs inside and empty them into your bowls and fill your water bowls too."

"Thank you so much, Queen and Spindle. I can't believe how delicious your food is. I am getting addicted to it."

"I'm happy to hear that, Madrigal. Where is Izara?"

"She is at the back of the lair hiding out. She is sulking more likely. Don't worry. When she smells this delicious food, she will come quickly. I assure you!"

Before the Queen could finish filling the bowls and water, Izara was there waiting to eat.

Madrigal grinned at the Queen and winked. "See, I told you!" he laughed.

Spindle picked up the empty tubs to assist Queen Solinara to bring them back to her workshop. He smiled when he saw the four dragons devouring their meals.

Queen Solinara and Spindle observed Izara as she burped after her last mouthful. They waited to see how she would react.

"Are you full, Izara?" Queen Solinara asked.

Izara raised her eyes to look at the Queen and sighed, "I am sated, Queen. That was the most delicious of all meals that you have served us. I am deeply grateful to you."

Queen Solinara grinned and nodded to Izara and left the lair. She whispered, "I think it worked, Spindle."

"I think so, Queen. I never doubted your expertise," Spindle smiled as they flew back to the Queen's workshop.

King Gateskin met them as they came back. "What's going on, you two?"

Queen Solinara explained what she had just done with the food for the dragons and how Izara was more agreeable when spoken to.

"That's good to hear, dear. I knew you would be able to handle the toughest dragon."

The dragon ladies came out of the house after taking a nap and asked if their dragons were behaving themselves. Their days of training had been grueling causing them to take naps each day.

"No worries, ladies. The Queen took care of any issues."

The dragon ladies raised their eyes and wondered what the dragons were up to now. They went to the lair to find out.

CHAPTER FORTY-TWO

Back in Parotovina, the King went in search of his queen who was avoiding him. He knocked on her workshop door and waited.

"Beregina, are you in there? Why are you ignoring me? I have been calling you. I wanted to discuss something about the dragons and your potion."

Beregina did not answer and waited for Kaposkaran to go away. He kept knocking and calling out to her. She finally opened the door and gave him a look of displeasure.

"We need to discuss this. You evidently knew that this was not going to work. Why did you not tell me?"

The Queen ignored him and turned to close the door but the King put his foot in the way preventing that.

"Why don't you want to explain what happened? I'm sure you can figure out what to do to fix this."

"I don't want to discuss it!"

"You have no choice, Beregina. You are the only one who can fix this. You have the powers of your spells and potions. You need to do something to make this work. If you don't, we are lost here."

"What do you want me to do, Kaposkaran? I have tried everything to fix it since I noticed the negative results. I will keep working on it. I don't need you to constantly bother me. Let me work on it." Beregina turned and closed the door with finality.

King Kaposkaran stood there with his mouth open and turned to leave. He was at a loss to say anything more to her and didn't know what else to do. All he could do was wait and hope that she would figure out the problem with her potion.

He instructed his men to dispose of the burnt remnants and clean the large cart. He planned to use this cart again with more success the next time.

The guards grumbled and tried to hold their noses as they picked up the burnt Catlings and disposed of them in a large container with a lid. They placed it far away from the village and proceeded to clean the cart as per the King's instructions. They did not understand any of this and felt lost. They knew something strange had happened on their previous mission and now this one but couldn't remember everything. They did not want to return for fear of something else happening to them preventing them from returning home.

The King had told them to go home once they had completed their tasks. They were relieved and exhausted but still confused. If anyone had asked them what they did or how it all happened, they couldn't explain. This is what bothered them the most.

Queen Beregina picked up some more bugs outside in the garden and brought them inside to her workshop. She would try another potion on these new bugs and see what happened. She had to discover what was wrong and fix it for the next mission that her husband said was to take place soon. She would prove herself once and for all.

***

Back in Sovorotskina, King Gateskin was preparing for more problems ahead from King Kaposkaran. He knew that the man would not stop at defeat and would keep trying to disrupt his training of the dragons. This time, Gateskin knew that Kaposkaran's mission would be to steal one or both of his dragons. He thought over what he would do to prevent this from happening.

Gateskin called to order Spindle, Mitteran and all his men. He sent out a message to Hotenfaran and Procelina, his brother-in-law and wife, a powerful wizard and fairy, his four Wizards, and Henno and Jenara, a powerful pair from Parotovina, who sought asylum in Sovorotskina. He would need all the power and magic he could muster to meet whatever was coming his way from Parotovina.

Everyone was settled in his conference room which he had to extend with a little bit of magic spells to accompany them. He went around the table after explaining what might be coming their way.

"Kaposkaran will be pulling out all his tricks and potions that his wife, Beregina, could create to send our way. We must be ready with our own powers and magic to meet them head on. Do you think you can handle this onslaught?"

"He doesn't have any powerful people in the village anymore. They have all hidden away or escaped to other villages as we have," Henno explained.

"Yes, that is true, but his wife is powerful and dangerous when she uses Dark Magic as we know she has done in the past," Gateskin agreed.

"Yes, I have seen this magic with the Moss Spell. There is evidence still of some deep inside the UT to this day. It doesn't spread much though since the animals there eat it," Spindle stated. This information he had gleaned from his fellow Sprites.

"As long as it doesn't come this way," Mitteran added.

"We will know how to handle it if it does, Mitteran. I am not worried about that. I do think, not worry, about what Beregina has up her powerful sleeves," the King stated with a frown.

Hotenfaran stood up and said, "We have more than enough magic here in this room, Gateskin. I don't think we have to worry about much. Besides us we also have four dragons on site."

"Yes, we do, Hotenfaran. I did not forget about them," Gateskin said with a grin as he looked toward the dragon ladies who had just entered the room after a nap in their quarters.

"Sorry, we didn't want to disturb you, King. We did hear you mention our dragons. They are here at your disposal as always. We still have a few days left of the training. Our father does not expect us back to report our results yet," Aharona replied.

"I appreciate that, Aharona, thank you," Gateskin answered and offered them a seat at the extended conference table to join in the discussion at hand.

"We don't need to interfere with your discussion, King. We can excuse ourselves and visit with the dragons," Navaeha announced.

"No, please stay. We may need your consul about what the dragons can do for us in this particular situation, King Gateskin explained.

"Okay," the dragon ladies agreed jointly, out of curiosity.

CHAPTER FORTY-THREE

The four dragons roamed around their lair and grunted in boredom and hunger as always. They never had enough to eat. They wondered what time it was and if it was almost time for another meal.

Izara was napping or trying to while the other three grunted and groaned their discomfort. They were told to stay put for now until their mistresses and the King came to fetch them. They didn't have any concept of time but were impatient if it took even a few minutes to be summoned.

The wolves could sense the discomfort of the dragons and kept their young inside their huts for safety. They did not trust the dragons to behave when they were hungry.

The Quintaroons looked out their windows and could sense something was afoot. They were getting restless too and needed to get outside for their daily walk and fresh air. They had tried on numerous occasions to open their windows and escape somehow, to no avail. That wouldn't stop them from trying.

One particular villager known as Botular, previously from Parotovina known as the eyes and ears of King Kaposkaran, had been quiet for some time. He emerged from his place in the village to poke his nose into what was happening. He had been watching at a distance while the King trained the dragons. He was fascinated and wanted to see them up close but was a little hesitant to do that. He would stay on the outskirts and watch.

***

Aharona and Navaeha excused themselves when they noticed how long they had been at the conference table with the King and others. They were concerned about the dragons getting antsy and into mischief.

They went in search of Queen Solinara who was in her workshop mixing more food for the dragons and wolves simultaneously. She looked up from her work when she saw the ladies standing there.

"Is everything all right, ladies?"

"Oh, yes. We were coming to fetch some food for our hungry dragons. We fear they are getting restless if they don't have a snack or two all day long," Aharona pointed out.

"I am in the process of preparing a tub of food for each of them now. I will have my children fly it over to the lair shortly. The tubs are much too heavy for you to carry that far. Serena and Simon can fly it over."

"That would be fine. In the meantime, we will go see how they are doing and inform them that food is on the way," Navaeha noted with a sigh of relief.

Serena and Simon were summoned by their mother with Catalina along to assist. Being the youngest sibling was always an issue for her. Catalina had to work harder to keep up with her sister and brother. She did not fly but could blend into her surroundings or become invisible even though she was working on learning how to fly as Serena had.

Each sibling had their own powers. Serena could move objects with her mind, read minds, and now fly while Simon could fly.

Simon had offered to teach Catalina how to fly as he had Serena. It took a little magic and a spell or two to work. Sometimes though it could wear off. They had to be careful of that. He would have to warn both his sisters about that fact.

The three arrived at their mother's workshop and were given instructions to bring the food to the hungry dragons right away.

"No problem, Mother," Serena retorted as her siblings nodded in agreement.

"I can't believe how much they eat!" Catalina exclaimed in a snicker.

"Maybe you better keep your distance, Catalina. You would make a tasty snack for them," Simon teased.

His sister stuck out her tongue and turned away to ignore him.

The dragon ladies had already headed over to the lair to alert the dragons that food was on its way and to ensure that their charges were behaving themselves until it arrived.

Catalina picked up a tub and grunted at its weight. She was surprisingly strong but would not be able to walk the food over without the help of her siblings and a little magic.

"Don't try to lift it, Catalina. Let me put a spell on it to lighten the load. It is heavy for all of us. You can hold onto my hand and we will fly together with the tubs in between us. The magic will last until we arrive at the lair. Now give me your hand and let me lift you and the tub," Serena implored.

Catalina giggled with delight as she floated up beside her siblings and held on to her sister with one hand while she held the tub with the other. Simon laughed at the joy on his younger sister's face as the three flew over to the lair.

Aharona and Navaeha came out of the lair when they heard the children call them.

"We are here. Do you want to let the dragons know we will come inside and deliver their food. We don't want to wake or startle them," Serena announced.

The dragons had heard Serena's voice and poked their heads out at the top of the lair.

"Please come in, children. You are always welcome when you have food for us," Madrigal remarked with a grin.

The four dragons moved aside and eagerly waited for the children to fill their bowls to the top. Simon and Serena picked up the water bowls and refilled them from the spring nearby, placed them down as quickly as they could and backed away giving the dragons room to eat.

They watched in awe as the dragons devoured the food and licked their jaws that were dripping from saliva, ending with several burps of pleasure.

Serena laughed along with her siblings and said, "I guess that means that it was satisfactory."

"Most definitely, Princess," Callum stated with a grin as the other dragons nodded with broad smiles.

"We will give our mother your compliments," Simon added as he chuckled.

"Please do, Prince," Evander bowed to the children.

The dragon ladies waited until the dragons were settled once again and napping before leaving them to return to see the King.

Serena's ears picked up a sound from the direction of the path leading to the Quintaroons' house. She turned to her siblings and whispered, "Did you hear that?"

Simon nodded and so did Catalina.

"Maybe we better check that out. It could be the Quintaroons trying to get out of their house again. Spindle told me about them doing something with the window in the bathing room," Serena declared with urgency.

"We can fly over so that they won't see us," Simon suggested. "Come, Catalina, I will pull you up here and hold onto you."

"Thank you, Simon. I like flying. You must train me to do this on my own. Can we start soon?" Catalina urged.

"Yes, but now do it this way. We need to help Serena with the Quintaroons. I will put a spell on you to assist in keeping you in the air. First, I just need to pull you up here with us."

"Okay, pull away," Catalina whooped with glee.

The three flew as fast as they could to seek the sounds that they heard ahead. They flew over and around the Quintaroons' house to see if there was any sign of their escaping.

"I don't see anything out of the ordinary," Simon stated, "Do you, Serena."

"No, I don't either. I am going to knock on the door and see if they are there. If they don't answer, that would be the problem."

"What are we going to do if they don't answer, Serena?" Catalina implored.

"Wait. Let's see if they answer first," Serena suggested.

The three waited for a few minutes and knocked again. It took several more minutes and another knock before the door could be opened, after Serena released the Lock Spell. The two Quintaroons stood there looking confused.

"What is wrong, Princess?" Quintal asked with a frown.

"Are you all right?" Serena asked.

"We…we…are fine," Talon stammered.

"Are you sure about that?" Simon stressed.

"Of course, why wouldn't we be okay?" Quintal answered.

"We heard a funny sound coming from here like something was breaking. Did you break something?" Serena interrogated.

"Oh no…nothing was broken, Serena," Talon responded with a nervous tic.

"Can we come in and inspect that everything is as you say, Quintal?" Serena implored.

"Well, of course, you can. Come in all of you," Quintal stated and stepped aside to allow them to enter.

Talon moved along with the children from room to room and watched them closely. He stood in front of the bathing room window and tried to block it.

"Move aside please, Talon," Serena instructed.

"There is nothing to see here, Princess," Talon insisted.

The children's eyes grew wide when they saw what the Quintaroons had done.

CHAPTER FORTY-FOUR

The King and his court and Wizards were wrapping up their discussions and plans for when King Kaposkaran's men returned to wreak havoc once again as the children rushed inside out of breath.

"What's going on, you three?" Gateskin asked.

Serena explained what she and her siblings had witnessed in the Quintaroon's house. "We put a spell on it to prevent them from escaping until you could see it for yourself, Father."

"Why did you go to their house? It could have been dangerous."

"Sorry, Father. We weren't thinking about that. We were worried that they would have escaped to cause trouble, especially with the dragons."

"Hmm, I see. Well, I guess I will have to go inspect this for myself." Turning to Spindle and Mitteran, he added, "Come with me. I may need your assistance to fix the damage."

Gateskin and his Head Guards flew to the house in question to do their inspection. The children were instructed to stay behind.

"Are you sure, Father? We can help," Serena pleaded.

"Yes, I am sure. I think you did enough already. Now go see if you mother needs assistance feeding the other animals."

"Yes, Father," Serena consented and nodded to her siblings to follow her.

When Gateskin, Spindle, and Mitteran arrived at the Quintaroons' house they didn't need to knock on the door because the two culprits were watching out the window expecting their arrival. After Gateskin released the Lock Spell, the door could be opened as they stepped onto the threshold. The King had given Spindle a key to use if he was not with him since Spindle did not know the spell or how to use it.

Gateskin looked at the Quintaroons with a stern expression of disapproval. He didn't need to utter a word for the Quintaroons hung their heads in shame for what they had done.

They led the way for the King and his guards to the area in question. They backed away for the King to inspect the damage they had incurred on the window and wall.

The King shook his head back and forth as he looked at the gaping hole in the wall, the missing slates of wood that held up the frame of the window and the floor that was littered with all this destruction.

"What were you planning to do when you escaped?" King Gateskin questioned the perpetrators.

"Umm…we only wanted to get some fresh air and take our daily walk, King," Quintal mumbled with his head down, not meeting the stony gaze of the King.

Talon just looked guilty and shrugged his shoulders when the King looked his way.

"You will fix this yourselves with the guidance of Spindle and Mitteran," King Gateskin instructed.

"Yes, King. We will fix it right away. Please forgive us. We did not want to anger you. You have been kind and considerate, allowing us to stay here and fixing us so that we can live as humans again," Quintal continued.

"Once you have completed this job to the satisfaction of my two Head Guards, you will be escorted for a walk and returned to your house under arrest. Do you understand?"

"Yes, of course, King. We understand perfectly," Talon interjected with a heavy sigh.

Spindle nodded and he and Mitteran began to instruct the startled Quintaroons what to do to fix the mess they had created.

Gateskin turned and left their house to return to other more pressing matters of concern. He sighed and kept shaking his head in disbelief as he mumbled to himself, "I can't believe they did this! I will have to keep a closer eye on them at all times."

After the damage was repaired, Spindle and Mitteran took the Quintaroons for their walk and kept these creature-men in their sights as they flew above them.

The Quintaroons were fearful of saying a word to each other and getting into more trouble with their schemes of escape. There would be another time for them to try something different. What they did notice was Spindle's sword hanging from his belt. Talon asked Quintal, "Do you think Spindle will use that on us?"

"I hope not. It may be small but Spindle is one powerful Sprite. We better watch ourselves."

Spindle and Mitteran discussed this latest episode of destruction by the Quintaroons and snorted in disbelief how brazen these creatures could be. They were definitely not to be trusted.

Mitteran agreed to stay close to the Quintaroons' house as Spindle went to report to the King that the problem was handled satisfactorily.

Serena looked up from the wolves' huts when she spotted Spindle coming her way.

"Hi Spindle. Is everything okay now? Did they fix the damage?"

"Yes, we instructed them how to do that and made sure it was reinforced so it couldn't happen again. I need to speak with your father. Is he inside?"

"Yes, I think he is," Serena sent an air kiss to an embarrassed Sprite who snatched it out of the air and hurried on his way to see the King.

King Gateskin witnessed this display of affection between his daughter and Spindle and smiled. He thought, "What am I going to do with those two?"

He turned away from the window when he heard Spindle at the door. "Come in, Spindle. Did it go well?"

"Yes, King. Everything is back to normal and we took them for their walk. We can bring them their dinner when it is time. Mitteran is standing guard to ensure they don't try something else."

"Good to hear. You are both good men. I am pleased with how you handled the situation."

"My pleasure, King," Spindle bowed his head as his face turned a shade of green after receiving the compliment.

"Do you want me to check in on the dragons again before I return home?"

"Yes, please do that. They were restless and I want to ensure that they are sated and hopefully sleeping off their full stomachs."

"Right away, King. I will report back if there are any problems. If not, you won't hear from me."

"Thank you, Spindle. Try to get some rest because tomorrow will most likely bring more problems for us to handle. Send Mitteran home too. Both of you have had long days."

Spindle saluted the King and flew on his way.

CHAPTER FORTY-FIVE

The two weeks had flown by since the training of the dragons began. This was the last day before the dragon ladies returned home to report that the dragons had passed the many tests they had given them. There was only one test left – the one that the dragons would allow King Gateskin to ride them around and obey his every command.

King Gateskin stood next to the ladies and waited for the dragons to come out of their lair. He smiled at them and received one smile in return from Madrigal and only a smirk from Izara who was feeling a little testy this morning.

Aharona stepped closer to Izara and whispered in her ear. Izara's head snapped up and she looked around. She looked a little startled by whatever Aharona had said to her.

Evander and Callum were nearby to provide backup in case Izara gave Aharona any trouble. They kept their eyes glued to the female dragon and nodded at her to listen.

King Gateskin spoke up, "Is everything okay, Aharona? Do you need me to come closer?"

"Not yet, King. Izara and I have a few things to discuss. She is almost ready for you. Why don't you ride Madrigal and give him some commands to obey. We will test him first," Aharona stressed.

Navaeha summoned Madrigal over to the King and let the King prepare to jump up onto the dragon's back to take their first flight together. Navaeha stepped back and gave them some room to take off.

Madrigal happily bent down to make it easier for the King to get on his back. He listened as the King gave him directions where to go and what to do. Madrigal nodded and flew up and soared over the village staying clear of any villagers who were out in their fields. He flew over the King's house and land, gliding smoothly and expertly around as he was commanded.

When they saw the King's children out in the field gathering vegetables, Madrigal dipped and waved at them as instructed by the King. They waved back amazed to see their father flying on the dragon's back. They called out to him, smiled and waved until Madrigal and the King had turned and flown back to the lair.

They were only gone for a short time when they landed in front of the lair and the King hopped off. Gateskin patted the dragon on his head and whispered something to him.

Izara watched every minute of the flight and tried to listen in to what the King was saying to her mate. She was still feeling a little out of sorts and not sure if she wanted to do this. Aharona had given her a warning that she could not ignore.

King Gateskin came closer to Izara and waited for her to look his way. He called out to her, "Izara, are you ready for our flight together?"

Izara was about to object until she heard a loud clearing of a throat belonging to Aharona that changed her mind. She met the King's eyes and nodded as she bent down for him to get onto her back.

They set off at a quick pace and circled the village as Madrigal had done only this time the King asked her to fly over the UT, high enough to stay away from the treetops and the Catlings who might be there.

Gateskin looked down at the forest and spotted a few Catlings who were looking up at them. These cats quickly scattered back to their dens in fear of dragons and their fiery breaths.

The King instructed Izara to fly over the wolves' huts and his home and fields. He commanded Izara to circle around again and repeat the flight before finally returning to the lair.

The whole time they were airborne, King Gateskin spoke to Izara and shared what he wanted to accomplish on his land and over all of Noella Province. Izara listened and nodded that she understood and made a soft landing in front of the others who were watching them.

King Gateskin whispered in Izara's ear, patted her on the head and stroked her purple wing. Izara purred and actually smiled at the King, much to his surprise and pleasure.

A delicious furry creature was presented to the dragons in thanks for successful flights. Of course, the other two dragons watched and waited for some treats too, which Gateskin was more than ready to provide for their assistance in all the training.

"That was most successful, King. Don't you agree?" Aharona and Navaeha asked.

"Yes, I do believe they were both successful flights. I think these dragons are going to be a wonderful addition to our home. I hope your father would agree with me."

"Oh, don't worry about that. We will convince him that it is the best thing he ever did to allow another land to have two dragons."

"Tell him that I will visit him soon on the dragons along with my wife. That is if I can convince her to ride one. If not her, I know that my oldest daughter will be more than willing to do so."

"I bet she will. The dragons like your children, King Gateskin, and so do we," Navaeha stated with a smile.

The four dragons were whispering amongst themselves about the flights.

Madrigal gave Izara a hug in thanks for her cooperation. "Nice job, Izara. I am proud of you. I know it has been difficult for you to adjust to our new home. I think we are going to be happy here. We have everything we could possibly want – a kind and caring master, delicious food and a beautiful lair in which to sleep. What more could we ask for?"

"I guess you are right, Madrigal. King Gateskin shared with me that he has great things he wants to accomplish with us. He said that he would give us everything we want in food and comfort in exchange for assistance in keeping this land safe."

"He did? He didn't say any of that to me. But I have been more agreeable than you have. I believe he had to convince you of how good this place could be. I was already convinced."

"Yes, I guess you are right. I will work harder to be more agreeable."

"That is good to hear, dear. I love you, you know that even when you are snarky."

"Who's snarky?" Izara exclaimed.

All Madrigal could do was laugh a hearty laugh over and over again as he held his sides.

The other two dragons heard the exchange and guffawed just as loud.

The dragon ladies and the King looked at the laughing dragons and shook their heads. "Now what is so funny?"

"I guess they have a private joke going on there," Aharona stated as she grinned, enjoying the dragons' gaiety.

"It's good to see them all so happy," Navaeha said as she sighed. "Maybe our dragons won't want to leave."

"Of course, they will, Navaeha. I'm not worried about that. We have to return home. We need to protect our family from you know who."

"Yes, I know. But I am liking it here more and more, Aharona."

King Gateskin heard the conversation between the sisters and didn't want to interrupt but said, "You know that you are all welcome to stay here as long as you want. I understand how important it is that you return home because of your sister. Always remember that you have a second home here with us. We will be here if you need us. You have another family here."

"Thank you, King Gateskin. I don't know how to show my gratitude," Aharona stressed.

"Yes, we appreciate your kindness, hospitality and friendship. It does feel like a home away from home. We will miss you all," Navaeha acquiesced.

"We feel the same about both of you. Oh, before I forget. Aharona, what did you whisper to Izara? She was suddenly more agreeable to me."

"Oh that, I just told her that I would take her back with us and get Madrigal another mate to live with him here."

"I guess she didn't like that at all," Gateskin snickered.

"You bet she didn't. She was testing me till the last second too. That is why I cleared my throat to let her know how serious I was," Aharona giggled.

"Well, I think we should get ready to return home. I'm sure our father is anxious to hear about the training," Navaeha added.

"Okay, please stop by and say goodbye to my wife and children. They will feel as sad as I feel and more so if you didn't see them before you leave. My wife will pack some refreshments for your long journey too."

"That is most kind of you, King. We will do that right away." The dragon ladies walked over to their dragons to announce that it was time to go home.

CHAPTER FORTY-SIX

On Dragonaria, King Marcellus and Queen Isla were pacing back and forth in their huge sitting room.

Queen Isla sighed and asked, "Do you think our girls are coming back today? I hope they don't like Sovorotskina too much. They may not want to return home."

"Don't even say that, Isla. Of course they are going to return. This is their home and has been their whole lives. They love this island and everything in it."

"Yes, I agree, but King Gateskin is a benevolent ruler and has been most generous in his hospitality to our girls while they visited, especially since they were there the first time unannounced."

"I don't think he minded that since he benefitted in a great way with the dragons. Our girls also helped him by using their dragons to dig for that thing they told us about," Marcellus reminded her.

"Oh, yes, you mean the chest with the Medallion," Isla sighed.

Several hours later, Aharona and Navaeha arrived home after dark. They went directly to their parents' home and were surprised to see they were not there.

"Now where did they go?" Aharona asked, looking around from room to room. She even called out to them.

"I hope Elowen hasn't been up to something again. Do you think she kidnapped them?" Navaeha asked, clearly stressed.

"No, I don't think she would be that inconsiderate."

"You don't? What about when they were trapped in the basement in cages with the staff? Who do you think did that?"

"I'd like to think that she did not do that. Maybe Father has other enemies or someone who wants his riches and power." Aharona stated with a frown.

"They said nothing was stolen. There were masked men who entered the castle. Who could have done that? None of the islanders would want to harm our parents."

"We may never know. We will have to keep an eye out and stay close by with our dragons to ensure that doesn't happen again."

"I'll go upstairs, Aharona. Maybe they went to bed and didn't hear us come in."

"Okay. I will check the other rooms and the basement just in case."

Navaeha entered her parents' bedroom and saw them in bed fast asleep. She left quietly and raced down the stairs to report to her sister that they were safe.

Aharona was down in the basement looking in every corner when she heard her sister's voice.

"Where were you, Aharona?"

"I was in the basement. Did you find them? Are they all right?"

"Yes, they are fast asleep and evidently heavy sleepers. We can stay in our old rooms tonight and be here when they wake up. I will let the dragons go to their dens so they can rest too. No need to keep them here," Navaeha announced as she left the castle.

***

Elowen watched her sisters return and hurried back to her house. She had put a spell on her parents to keep them sleeping. She planned on taking over the castle and becoming the new queen. She was hoping that her sisters were not going to return, being so enamored with King Gateskin and his land.

She called her charges, men who she had put a spell on to keep them in her control. It had worked before when they had entered the castle and caged her parents and the staff. If her sisters hadn't returned and messed everything up, she would have had control of the island and its people. She would work on getting control of all the dragons too. That would take extra doses of Dark Magic though.

Back in the castle her sisters fell asleep and didn't wake until the next morning. They heard the staff preparing for the day with breakfast. They peeked into their parents' room but they were still in bed. They tiptoed out and went downstairs to have breakfast.

When the staff saw them, they rushed over to hug and offer them a dish full of food as if they had been gone forever.

"We are fine, Matilda. We can't eat that much. Are you trying to fatten us up?" Aharona bantered.

"Oh no, Princesses, we are just happy to see you, that is all. Your parents stayed up late waiting for you. I guess they are still sleeping."

"Yes, we checked on them. Maybe we should wake them up so that they can see we are home safe and sound," Navaeha debated.

"Let's eat something first. After we can go up there and wake them together," Aharona suggested, digging into the pancakes, eggs and bacon and fresh fruit.

"Okay, I am hungry too. We will be able to relate the results of the successful training better on full stomachs," Navaeha agreed.

"Do you think Father will be unhappy about the success King Gateskin had with the dragons, Navaeha?"

"No, I think he will be relieved that it is over. I don't think he will ever give up any more dragons to others though. He fears what other rulers will do with them. They may not be as kind as King Gateskin," Navaeha stated as she kept shoveling food into her mouth in between words.

"I certainly hope so, sister. I don't want to be here when he has one of his tirades again. Mother is the only one who can calm him down."

The ladies finished breakfast and still had not heard their parents moving about. They began to worry and hurried upstairs to check on them.

When they stepped inside the room, their parents were still in bed.

Aharona went over and whispered to them and shook them lightly without any results.

"Something is wrong, Aharona! They are not responding to us. They never sleep this late. Do you think Elowen had something to do with this?"

"I don't know, sister. I think we may need some help and a little magic from a friend."

Aharona remembered that King Gateskin said that if they ever needed him to just call out to him in their minds for help.

Aharona pulled her sister back downstairs and told her what they must do. They sat together on the divan and concentrated on Sovorotskina and the King and relayed that they were in dire need of his assistance.

In a matter of minutes if not seconds they heard the King's voice in their minds that he would be there as soon as he could.

King Gateskin had no idea what was going on in Dragonaria. He feared that King Marcellus was displeased with the success he had with the dragons and wanted them returned. If he traveled there on the backs of the dragons, he may have to leave them there and never get them back. He debated about this and spoke with his Head Guards, Spindle and Mitteran.

He planned to take Spindle with him and leave Mitteran in charge of everything at home until they could return. He only hoped that this was going to be a minor setback. But he couldn't imagine the ladies calling him with something minor. It must be quite serious for them to need him right away. Their request was intense and definitely filled with fear and worry.

He sent his thoughts back to them. "Are either of you in danger? Is it Elowen? Is she the problem? Are your parents harmed?"

Gateskin received the urgent message that something was wrong with their parents and they urgently needed his help. They didn't know who had done this to their parents for they couldn't be awakened from a deep sleep.

The King knew by the sounds of this that it was Dark Magic that had to be responsible and most likely Elowen was behind it.

He also summoned Hotenfaran and Procelina to watch over his family until his return, explaining what he thought the issue on Dragonaria could be. He also sent mind messages to Henno and Jenara who had powers that could be useful to come along with him and Spindle.

As Gateskin prepared to travel to Dragonaria on a mission of support and possible rescue of King Marcellus and Queen Isla, he prepped Spindle and Henno and Jenara on what to expect. He also enlisted four more guards to back him up on the trip. He would supply them with magic to enable them to fly alongside him and the rest of the group.

The King was prepared for whatever was ahead of them on this island. He only hoped that no one was injured on this mission.

CHAPTER FORTY-SEVEN

Gateskin sent a message to the dragon ladies
that he was on his way and would do his best to
be there as soon as possible with a heavy dose
of magic.

The ladies sighed in relief when they heard the
King's words. This did not stop them from

pacing back and forth though much to the dismay of Matilda who was in the kitchen preparing lunch for the group and poking her head into the living area to check on Aharona and Navaeha in between her tasks. She shook her head and mumbled to herself that she was disappointed in Elowen and her shameful ways. Imagine a daughter trying to harm her own parents. That was unconscionable.

Matilda's thoughts were disturbed when Navaeha came into the kitchen and requested a pot of tea for herself and her sister to help calm them down.

"Are you all right, Navaeha? Is Aharona?"

"Well, we are nervous and will be that way until King Gateskin arrives to help us. I only pray that he can do something to lift the spell off our parents. They can't be like that forever? What are we going to do if they are?"

"No, they will not be that way forever, Navaeha. Your friend, King Gateskin, looks like a kind and powerful man. He will find a way to counteract the spell of your sister, Elowen. I can't believe she would do such a thing! I am disappointed in her. She wasn't always like this as a child. I remember when she was sweet and always rambunctious. When you two came along is when she changed for the worse. I guess maybe it was jealousy. She was no longer the only child and did not receive as much attention after that."

"I'm sorry to hear that, Matilda. We were too young to understand or notice that. We looked up to her though because she was smart and beautiful and we wanted to be just like her when we grew up. Now not so much," Navaeha said with a sigh.

"I will bring you a pot of tea and some of my cookies that you love. I just took them out of the oven."

"I can smell them, Matilda. Thank you so much. We wouldn't know what to do without you. You have been like a second mother to us."

"Ah, no worries, child. I am here to help you in any way I can, even if it is just to be a mother until your mother returns." Matilda tried to keep her tears at bay at Navaeha's kind words. She did want to be a mother only if she could have lovely daughters like Navaeha and Aharona.

Aharona was at the front windows looking at the sky and sighing. "Where are they?"

Navaeha stood next to her and said, "It's only been a short time since we received the King's message. Maybe it was half an hour ago at the most, Sister. It's at least a two-hour journey without the assistance of magic. The winds can be fierce at times and blow you aside making it difficult to travel in a straight line."

"I know, but I am so anxious," Aharona retorted.

"Matilda is making us a pot of tea and will bring it in shortly along with her molasses cookies that I love with the raisins. They smell so good."

"Don't you ever think of anything except food, Navaeha?"

"Yes, of course I do. I think of a lot of things. When I am nervous, I think of food more and find it soothes me. There's nothing wrong with that, is there?"

"I guess not. No food could soothe me until this is over," Aharona grumbled.

"I understand, Sister. Please sit down and have some tea. Here is Matilda with the tea and cookies."

"Thank you so much, Matilda. We appreciate you in so many ways," Aharona stated with a wane smile.

"No problem, Aharona. I am here to aid you in any way I can as I told your sister. Please don't worry too much, all will work out. I know it will."

"I hope so, Matilda. Thank you. I will try to relax. I'm sure King Gateskin will find a way to make this right."

Matilda nodded and gave the girls her sweetest smile as she went back to her domain.

***

King Gateskin and company whipped through the air with the aid of a few magic spells. They had to keep close together for them to work. The guards looked a little leery about the fast travel. The guards had never done this before but were bolstered by Spindle to be brave and hold onto each other and stay next to him.

"You are doing wonderfully, men. We will be there shortly thanks to the King's magic. Travel never was this fast. You will be able to take a deep breath when we land. Look ahead, there is the island now coming into view. It is so small compared to our province but it is quite beautiful with all the palm trees and the blue ocean all around."

The guards nodded, unable to respond until they had their feet firmly planted once again on land. They looked frightened, pale and out of their minds.

Spindle snickered at the look on their faces but didn't say anything to deter them from moving along. He sent a message to Gateskin, "We are almost there. Do you want me to go inside the castle with you and the others and leave the men outside to guard the front?"

"Yes, that would be a good idea, Spindle. That is why I chose you to be my Head Guard. You are always thinking ahead," Gateskin chuckled.

The dragon ladies were outside waiting for the group to land and looking anxious but relieved to see them.

Aharona stepped up to the group and spoke to the King, "We are so relieved to see you and can't thank you enough for coming all this way."

"It is my pleasure, Aharona. I told you both that you are like family to us and we always protect and aid our family."

"I…I…appreciate that," Aharona exhaled.

"Yes, King. We can't thank you enough. Do you know what can be done to bring our parents back?" Navaeha implored.

"I need to see them and make an assessment of the situation. It could be more complicated or it could be simple enough to do." Looking at Spindle, he beckoned him to come with him along with Henno and Jenara.

"I hope it is not too complicated. We have no idea what Elowen did to put them under this spell. It could last forever!" Navaeha wailed.

Aharona put her arms around her sister and calmed her down now. "Let's go inside so the King can see our parents and proceed. You need to keep it together."

"Yes, I'm sorry. I am so worried that…"

"I know, Navaeha. Get yourself another cookie. That should calm you down."

"Yes, I think that might do it. I can offer some to the guards too. I'm sure they are hungry for a snack after their long journey."

"Good, you do that, Navaeha. I will go upstairs with King Gateskin. Maybe I can help him."

Navaeha went outside to hand out cookies to the guards who hungrily accepted them. The snack appeared to calm them down too which made Navaeha smile and relax some more while she asked them how their journey was.

The guards rolled their eyes as they took another cookie and sighed.

Gateskin was upstairs assessing the sleeping King and Queen along with Spindle, Henno and Jenara. He spoke to the three in their minds and asked, "What do you think? Should we combine our spells at the same time or one spell at a time?"

Henno looked at Jenara and said, "I think we should try your spells first, King. If you need ours, we will step forward and apply them."

"I think I have one that might work. It would be like awakening the cattle from the Moss Spell in reverse."

"Hmm, that is interesting," Spindle added, as he hovered above the sleeping couple.

Gateskin spread his arms out over them and hummed and chanted. He waited a minute and did it again. The couple moved a little but did not awaken.

He turned to Henno and Jenara. "Now add your spells to this and we can be stronger together. This spell they are under is Dark Magic and quite stubborn. It will not be easy to break."

Henno and Jenara chanted and flew up above the couple and spread their magic around the bed and under it to cover all.

The couple began to move and rock back and forth in the bed banging into each other. The bed began to shake and levitate a few inches off the floor.

Spindle added his own Sprite magic at the request of the King and they stepped back and waited.

A dark cloud rose off the bodies as the couple began to mumble and sit up in bed.

King Marcellus opened his eyes first and looked around startled to see these people looking back at him.

"What happened? Why are you here?"

Before Gateskin could explain, Queen Isla sat up and cried out in alarm, "What's going on? Why are you all in our bedroom?"

"We want an explanation right away," King Marcellus snapped.

King Gateskin began to explain while King Marcellus' expression became more confused as his eyes grew wider in disbelief.

"Do you mean to say that Elowen put us to sleep? Why would she do that? What would she gain from this?"

"I don't know, King. She must have something planned. Maybe she wants to become leader of the island," King Gateskin suggested.

Aharona was outside the door when she heard her parents' angry voices. She rushed in to hug them and wept tears of relief.

Navaeha heard the commotion and hurried upstairs to see her parents and her sister crying together. She quickly joined them.

CHAPTER FORTY-EIGHT

After much discussion King Marcellus and Queen Isla agreed that it must have been Elowen who had put them to sleep. They were shaken by this development but at the time had come to terms that their eldest daughter was truly taken over by her use of Dark Magic. They thought over what had happened to them before when they had been locked in cages down in their basement.

Queen Isla shed tears as she hugged her two younger daughters who tried to calm and console her. She said through her tears, "What are we going to do about Elowen?"

Marcellus looked at his wife, his own eyes brimming with unshed tears and said, "We will get her back no matter what we have to do. We can't let Dark Magic take her from us."

Queen Isla nodded and wiped her tears away and sighed.

Aharona and Navaeha turned their gazes toward King Gateskin who had stood there listening to all their fears. "I will help you in any way I can. This may take some assistance from our dragons, don't you think, ladies?"

"Absolutely, King. Do you want us to go back with you to get them?"

"Oh no, I will do this on my own. Spindle will stay here with the guards to watch over you until I return. Henno and Jenara can come back with me."

Henno and Jenara followed the King out of the castle. They flew into the air and made a hasty retreat home to get some help.

Henno spoke to the King in his head since it was too difficult to speak out loud with the strong gusts of wind at their faces. "How can we assist you, King Gateskin?"

"I am working that out now. I need to speak to the dragons and let them know the problem we have. They will understand what to do since it is or was their home. They also know Elowen and how she fears dragons and their powers."

"Ah, I see. If we have four dragons to face her, she may capitulate."

"I am planning on that. She knows what she has planned. I'm positive she knows that we will come after her. She will be ready, I'm sure."

Jenara spoke up in the middle of their conversation to add something of her own. "What about your Quintaroons? Can they help in some way, King?"

"Now that is something to ponder, Jenara. Thank you. I will have a discussion with them. They have been up to mischief lately probably because they are bored. They may enjoy doing something productive instead of destructive."

Once they arrived back in Noella Province, the three went directly to King Gateskin's home to let his family know what had developed. Gateskin knew his wife would have something to add.

Queen Solinara was feeding their children and her brother and sister-in-law when Gateskin walked in. They all jumped up and hugged him saying, "Are you all right? What happened?"

Gateskin raised his hands to calm everyone and told them to sit down and he would explain. He told them about how the King and Queen of Dragonaria were now awake after a long sleep induced by the Dark Magic of their eldest daughter, Elowen. He also discussed his plans to use the dragons and possibly the Quintaroons after a suggestion by Jenara to do so.

"Do you think the Quintaroons will be more of a hindrance than a help, Gateskin?" Solinara voiced her concern.

"I am concerned about their recent behavior. I think they are bored and need to do something meaningful."

"Yes, I can see that may get them out of their boredom and mischievous ways, Gateskin."

Hotenfaran and Procelina spoke up, "Can we be of assistance, King?"

"Yes, you can. You can stay here to provide protection to my family. I don't like to be away too long."

"Of course, we will stay here and keep watch. We can assist with feeding the animals and helping your wife in any way we can," Procelina added.

"I can help you too, King," Arubane, son of Hotenfaran and Procelina, stated, with a serious face.

"I know you can, Arubane. But I think it would be better for you to stay to protect my children."

"I am honored to do that, King," he said as he went to find the children in their rooms to report that he would fulfil this duty.

Solinara raised her brows to them, "You all know that I am quite capable of handling everything myself including protecting myself and the children."

"Yes, dear. I am very well aware of that. Please do this as a courtesy to me. I worry about all of you. Just knowing that you are not alone will give me some peace and allow me to focus on the issues at hand on Dragonaria."

"All right, Gateskin. We will be fine here. You need not worry about anything. Just take care of the problems on Dragonaria and come back safe and sound, all of you. Do you hear me?"

"I always hear you, Solinara, my love. I listen all the time to your advice, do I not?"

"You had better listen and come back safely or I will worry." Solinara wrapped her arms around her husband's neck and whispered some endearments that brought a smile to his face.

"Well, we had better get a move on. We have lots to do. I need to discuss this with the dragons and the Quintaroons."

Henno and Jenara went over to Queen Solinara and said, "Don't worry, Queen. We will always have his back."

"Thank you, both. Stay safe."

"We plan to, Queen. We love it here in Sovorotskina and are indebted to you and the King for giving us asylum and a new life," Jenara stressed and bowed to the Queen.

The children raced after their father and hugged him and whispered, "Please be careful and come back to us. We will miss you and love you so much, Father."

He hugged them back and said, "I love you all so much too," Gateskin felt tears forming in his eyes. He wiped them away and headed toward the dragons' lair.

CHAPTER FORTY-NINE

Gateskin went to the dragons' lair to find the dragons sleeping. He made enough noise to awaken them and asked them to listen to what he had to say, for it was of the utmost importance.

Madrigal's eyes grew wider with each word spoken by the King while Izara did not meet the King's eyes.

"Well, what do you think about helping me with Elowen?" the King asked.

Madrigal stepped closer to the King and bowed. "I am at your service, good king. I will do whatever you need me to do to solve this problem once and for all. Elowen is nothing but trouble and will continue to be so."

"Thank you, Madrigal, for your support. You are an honorable dragon." Turning to Izara, he asked, "What about you, Izara? What do you think about this plan?"

"I don't know, King. I do know that Elowen is dangerous and can do much harm to the island and evidently has done that already. I don't want to see her harm the King and Queen there. They were always kind to all dragons and allowed us to stay there without any problems. I guess there is nothing else to do but go with you and assist in any way I can."

"That is good to hear, Izara. Thank you. You are also an honorable dragon and I feel grateful to have both of you by my side."

Henno and Jenara stayed at the back until the dragons came out. They did not want to get in the way. They had not yet met the dragons officially.

Gateskin introduced the dragons to the two powerful people standing there. The dragons blinked and waved their wings in response and Madrigal said, "We are honored to meet you both. Are you going to travel with us? You are both welcome to ride on my back while Izara can take the King, if that is all right with him."

King Gateskin nodded and said, "That is fine with me. Now let's go visit the Quintaroons."

On their way there Gateskin explained to the group that he would ask the Quintaroons to come along and use some of their powers to aid them in deterring Elowen from using her Dark Magic on them.

"Do these Quintaroons have powers to do that, King?" Madrigal queried.

"Yes, I think they do. They assisted us once before when Elowen visited our land unannounced. They can disappear if they drink water, shrink or grow in size if they eat…never mind about that one. They can fly and are formidable in size and strength. They even have dangerous claws and jaws just not as large as yours."

"My oh my, they do sound almost like us," Izara chuckled. "We better watch ourselves around them, huh, Madrigal?"

"Don't worry, dear one. I will be here to protect you," Madrigal grinned.

King Gateskin stepped up to the Quintaroons' door and knocked. In a matter of seconds, the door was opened by Quintal, once again after the Lock Spell was taken off by the King. Quintal looked around at the others who were gazing back at him.

"Well, what is going on here, King? Is this a special occasion that brings so many quests at once to our door?"

Talon looked over Quintal's shoulder at the group and reiterated, "What brings you all here today?"

Gateskin requested that they step outside for a meeting. "Please listen to what I have to say. This is most important and you must behave yourselves at all times. I will not stand for any insolence from either of you. Do you hear me?"

"Yes, of course, King. You are startling us, to say the least. What could be so dire?" Talon inquired.

Gateskin explained what had transpired on the island of Dragonaria to the King and Queen. He told them about who he suspected was the culprit to this dastardly deed.

The Quintaroons nodded with shocked expressions on their human faces. They listened and nodded some more as he explained what he wanted them to do.

"Does this mean we can change into our former selves, King?"

"Yes, you can do that in order to fly to the island. I can't carry you both. We only have two dragons and I am riding one and Henno and Jenara are riding the other. You would be too heavy to ride on either of the dragons once you change your forms."

"I see. Okay. How will we do this, King?" Quintal asked.

"Well, first of all you will concentrate as you did once before, Quintal, when you helped with Elowen another time. Do you remember what you did?"

"I don't remember everything I did. I do remember that horrid woman with her Dark Magic. I will do whatever you need me to do to stop her."

What Quintal did not know was that Queen Solinara helped him along at that time to make the transformation from human to creature with a little encouragement and a bit of magic of her own.

"Good. What about you, Talon? Are you willing to turn back to being a Quintaroon who will listen to your master?"

"You don't have to ask me twice, King. I've been wanting to…., I mean, I… Oh, never mind."

Quintal gave Talon a stern look at his almost gaffe.

"Well, let's begin, Quintaroons. Do your changing. We are in a hurry to return to Dragonaria. We cannot waste any time. Concentrate," King Gateskin urged. He recited a spell to help them along without their knowledge. He could also turn them back with this spell if he needed to curtail them in any way.

"Yes, sir, King. We are concentrating. I can feel something happening to me. Can you, Talon?"

"Yes, it is happening!" Talon whooped in delight.

Two large Quintaroons stood in place of the human forms and growled and became calm again when King Gateskin raised his hand to them to be silent.

"You will listen to my instructions at all times. Follow us to the island of Dragonaria and wait for further instructions. Do you understand?"

The Quintaroons nodded their heads and flew up behind the dragons and passengers to go to the island.

Spindle kept his eyes on the two creatures. He didn't trust them to behave. He only hoped that the King was not making a mistake taking them along.

He patted the sword at his belt and starred at the creatures in warning. They looked back at him and noticed his sword and exchanged wary looks with one another.

CHAPTER FIFTY

Aharona and Navaeha paced back and forth while they combed the skies looking for King Gateskin and the dragons.

"What is taking them so long?" Navaeha asked in exasperation.

"Stop worrying so much. You know King Gateskin had to convince the dragons to come. Maybe they are giving him a difficult time."

"Not Madrigal, but possibly Izara. She can be stubborn at times," Navaeha responded.

King Marcellus and Queen Isla were looking out their front windows and doing the same pacing. When they spotted the dragons coming, they raced out to meet them next to their daughters.

"Good to see you back, King Gateskin. Thank you for returning. We were wondering if the dragons were giving you a difficult time," King Marcellus stated as he looked at the dragons closely.

The dragons met King Marcellus' eyes and bowed. "We came to assist you, King. We would never have refused to come." Madrigal announced.

"That is a relief to hear. Thank you all for coming. Now, what is the plan?"

King Gateskin hopped down off Izara's back and came over to King Marcellus. "First thing, we don't need to keep calling each other king. We can use first names from now on. Is that all right with you, Marcellus?"

"Of course, Gateskin. It is a little more friendly-sounding since we are in this together." Turning to his daughters he said, "This only applies to us. You still need to call him King. Understand? It is only fair to give him respect."

"Yes, Father. We understand," his daughters agreed.

The two sisters looked at the creatures who were at the back of the dragons. "What? Who are those two?" Aharona asked.

"Oh, you haven't met our Quintaroons yet? They are in their creature form. You may have seen them when they were in human form."

"Ah, well, I don't think we did, King Gateskin. Why are they here?" Aharona asked, keeping an eye on them and staying a distance away.

"They really are large and fierce. Will they hurt us?" Navaeha asked as she too moved away.

"No, they will not harm you. They are under my control. No need to worry. Now let's discuss what we must do."

Gateskin gathered his group together and said, "Listen up, everyone. We must be alert and watchful for anything that Elowen may throw at us. We are going to visit her place but stay a distance away under my orders."

The dragons and the Quintaroons nodded along with Henno, Jenara, Spindle and the guards.

***

On the other side of the island, Elowen was preparing more spells to use. She had felt the disturbance in the air as the dragons and the strange creatures were heading her way. She didn't know what to expect but would be ready.

The dragons and Quintaroons landed in the area, a distance away, and lay low as they waited for word from King Gateskin what to do.

Elowen had set up a barrier near where they were standing and waited to see if they would move closer to be caught in her net of Dark Magic.

Gateskin, Henno and Jenara walked around the area and could feel the presence of the barrier. They told everyone to stay back and not move another foot or they would be caught in Elowen's magic spell.

The dragons whispered together, "What is this barrier that is here? Do you feel it?" Madrigal asked Callum and Evander who were sitting nearby.

"It is dangerous and can burn you or make you disappear. We have seen what she can do. Don't move a muscle. The King and his powerful people are conversing and we will know what they want us to do next. Be patient."

"I'm trying Callum. Sorry. This is all new to us. Even though this was our home, we never got near Elowen's property. We were warned to stay clear, and we did."

"You were smart to listen, Madrigal," Evander approved.

"Look, they are moving in!" Izara announced in a shocked and gravelly voice.

The four dragons watched to see if they were to follow as King Gateskin and Henno and Jenara moved closer to Elowen's house. As the three moved, they waved their hands and chanted spells to clean out the barrier of any danger to them all.

"It looks safe to move now," Madrigal announced.

"Wait, don't move yet," Evander stressed as he kept his eyes on the three.

"They are not being injured in any way," Madrigal continued.

"That is because they have used their powers to stop and clear the barriers as they move along, temporarily. If we move in too soon the barriers will affect us since we do not have the powers that the King has," Callum explained.

"I see what you mean. Look, the barrier is back in place right after they moved closer to her house. I can feel it," Madrigal added.

"If you had gone in you would be toast now," Callum said with a snicker.

"I wouldn't have followed you, Madrigal," Izara said as she shivered at the thought.

"You don't have to tell me more than once," Madrigal sighed and nodded to Callum.

King Gateskin and the powerful couple stopped outside Elowen's house and stepped up to knock at her door.

Elowen was watching them from her front window, clearly confused and upset. She opened the door and held her hands up to warn them off. "What are you doing here? How did you get through my barrier?"

King Gateskin smiled at Elowen to unsettle but also calm her. "We are not here to harm you. We want to talk about your father and mother."

"What about them?" Elowen asked as she kept her facial expression stoic.

"We know you put a spell on them to make them sleep. What your parents want to know is why you did that and also why you locked them up with their staff?"

"I...I...did not do any of that."

"Elowen?" King Marcellus called out to her from a safe distance.

"What?" Elowen responded, not meeting her father's eyes.

"Why? Don't you care for us at all? We have tried our best to provide for all our daughters and love you all."

"Hmm, is that right?"

"Yes, that is right," Queen Isla assured.

"Elowen, do you really want to take over our island from us? Don't you know that you and your sisters will be left to do this once we are gone. If you want to rule now, we can step aside but you must not use this Dark Magic. We will not allow that to destroy what we have built here."

Elowen didn't respond but raised her hands to send out a spell. King Gateskin and the powerful couple stopped the spell before it could reach King Marcellus and Queen Isla.

The King and Queen dropped down and were covered and protected by the four dragons who stepped up to help.

Evander and Callum were ready to unleash a blast of fire toward Elowen but King Marcellus stopped them.

"No, don't harm her, please. We need to work this out. I don't want anyone hurt," King Marcellus pleaded.

The two dragons bowed to their king and backed aside as King Marcellus called out to his daughter, "Whatever you want to do to me, do it. Don't harm anyone else."

Elowen put her hands down and shook her head. "I...I...don't want to hurt you, Father. I am angry and don't feel that you..."

"What? Please tell me, Elowen. I want to understand why you are so angry."

"I am alone here on our island. No one cares about me. The only thing I have is my Dark Magic. It makes me feel like I am important, that I matter. I don't matter to you and the rest of my family."

"How can you say that?" Isla stated in shock.

"Do you ask me to come to dinner? Do you have Matilda make my favorite things like you do for my sisters? Do any of you care about me?"

"We are afraid of your powers, Elowen. That is one reason why we stay away. Even now look at what you did to keep us away," her mother responded.

"I always have barriers up to keep me safe. I don't trust anyone or anything. I can see the hate in the eyes of your dragons. They were ready to burn me, weren't they?"

"They were only trying to protect me. I am their leader. If you were their leader, they would do the same thing."

"They would?"

"Yes, wouldn't you, Evander and Callum?" her father queried the dragons.

The two dragons exchanged puzzled looks with each other, sighed, and nodded in agreement when the King looked sharply at them.

"See, they would honor you as they do me. Now you need to stop this Dark Magic and come home for a celebratory dinner. What do you say?"

Elowen raised her hands causing everyone to drop down out of the way in fear as she disconnected the barrier around the area allowing everyone to come forward unharmed.

"I...I...will think about this, Father. You will not be harmed if you come closer now."

Her parents moved slowly toward the door as Elowen walked out of her house to meet them.

When they met, they embraced and cried on each other's shoulders.

Elowen looked over her parent's shoulders and eyed the strange creatures that were behind the dragons. She was curious about them and what powers they had. She smiled to herself behind her fake tears while plans began to develop in her mind about what she could do if she had them in her powers.

King Gateskin and the others moved away to give the family some privacy.

"Do you believe her, King Gateskin?" Henno and Jenara asked.

"I don't know but we must give her the benefit of the doubt. She may have changed her ways. We can only hope."

CHAPTER FIFTY-ONE

Gateskin sent a message to Solinara to let her know that all was well and that they would be home in an hour or so. He planned to speed up their return home with a little extra magic, much to the chagrin of his guards who shook all the way home and gripped each other's hands for stability and security. Their faces were quite green and sickly.

The two dragons were happy to return to Sovorotskina, their new home. They didn't say as much to each other but Madrigal could see the smile on his mate's face as they neared Noella Province.

After their arrival, the dragons bowed to King Gateskin and escaped to their lair for a much-needed nap and hopefully some food soon. When they entered their lair, they noticed their bowls were full of water and food much to their delight. After a quick meal and drink, they nodded off as they cuddled together.

Gateskin peeked inside the lair to make sure they were settled before leaving and escorting the Quintaroons back to their home after making sure they reverted back to their human forms. The Quintaroons also found some food was set out for them on their table and helped themselves as they bade goodbye to the King.

"Thank you for coming with me today. I'm sorry I didn't have anything for you to do but your presence there helped to speed things along with Elowen."

"Do you really think so, King?" Quintal asked.

"Most definitely. Well, enjoy your meal and get some rest. I'm sure you are tired from the trip. I will check in with you later."

"Thank you, King. We plan to do plenty of napping as soon as we eat all this delectable food the Queen left us. Please extend our gratitude to her," Talon added.

"Of course, I will." King Gateskin nodded to the Quintaroons, locked them safely inside, and headed home.

After the King left them, Talon announced his feelings about Elowen. "Did you notice that Elowen stared at us with a weird smile on her cruel lips while she was hugging her parents? Her tears were fake too. They dried up quickly."

"No, I didn't notice her looking at us or whether her tears were fake or not. I was more worried about the dragons, especially Evander. I don't think he likes us."

"Maybe he is a little leery about us and our powers. He may feel somewhat intimidated," Talon quipped. He looked at his food but could not eat because in his mind he could still see the weird, cruel smile on Elowen's lips causing him to shiver.

Quintal shrugged his shoulders and dug into his dinner with a heavy sigh unaware of his fellow Quintaroon's continued unease.

**

Solinara was standing at the door to welcome Gateskin home. Spindle bowed to the King and Queen while Henno and Jenara did the same.

"Thank you all for accompanying me. I'm relieved that it was not too dangerous for any of you. Go home and rest. We'll talk tomorrow."

"It was our pleasure, King. See you tomorrow," Henno and Jenara said.

"I'll see you tomorrow, King," Spindle added.

The three flew away to their respective homes.

Turning to his wife he said, "It's good to be home, Solinara."

"Yes, it's a relief to see you safely back, Gateskin," Hotenfaran and Procelina stated.

"It's good to have you here, Gateskin. I thought it would take much longer to convince Elowen to behave. What did you have to do? Please tell me everything. The children want to see you first though," Solinara stated with a little relief.

Before Gateskin could go to the children's rooms they came barreling out at him and hugged him furiously.

"Well, I guess that says it all. You missed me!" he laughed.

"Maybe just a little bit, Father," Serena stated with a wide grin and tears brimming in her eyes.

"What is this?" Gateskin wiped a tear off his daughter's cheek.

"Oh, I always worry about you. I know how dangerous Elowen is. I was fearful of her powers."

"You need not worry about your father, dear one. I have my powers and my guards and others at my side."

"I know you have one powerful Head Guard to protect you too," Serena giggled.

"Yes, him too!" Gateskin snickered.

Simon and Catalina waited their turn to talk to their father and quiz him on what had transpired.

"Did you kill Elowen, Father?" Simon asked.

"What? Kill her? Never! What made you think I would kill her, Simon?"

"I…I thought she might try to harm you and the others and you would be forced to do that."

"No, that would not happen, son. I am a benevolent king and would never kill anyone."

"Okay. So, what happened?"

"Yes, Father. We want to know everything," Catalina stressed with a serious expression.

"I was going to share that with your mother first and you later. Can you wait for a little while? Why don't you go check on the wolves and the barn animals in the meantime? Also, check the garden for some vegetables that are ready to be picked for dinner."

"All right. I guess we can wait." Solinara sighed and gestured to her siblings to follow her.

Solinara was preparing dinner when Gateskin returned to the kitchen and dining room after escorting his children outside.

"Hotenfaran, Procelina and Arubane left. They wanted to give us some time together to discuss your trip."

"They didn't have to do that, Solinara."

"I know. I told them that but they insisted. They have been here all day with me and needed to do some things at home."

"That was thoughtful of them but not necessary."

"Are you hungry, Gateskin?"

"Of course, I am always hungry, my love." Gateskin came up behind and hugged her as he kissed her neck.

Solinara sighed and snuggled close to him. "I like when you come back home after a mission. You are always more affectionate."

"Am I?" Gateskin guffawed as he held her tighter.

"Now tell me everything."

Gateskin relayed all that had transpired as Solinara continued to cook and nod at his every word.

"It looks kind of strange that Elowen would give up so easily. What do you think, dear?"

"Yes, my sentiments exactly, Solinara. I am worried about the safety of the whole island. I did send a message to the dragon ladies after we were almost home to let them know we are here if they need us again at a moment's notice."

"Good. They must be a little wary of their sister and her wily ways."

"I think they know her well enough to suspect that she is planning something else once she gets her parents' trust again."

"Dinner is ready. Call the children and I will set the table. I'm sure they are anxiously waiting to hear more," Solinara stated with a chuckle.

The children quickly came inside but had kept their ears peeled outside the window and heard every word their father had said. They didn't want him to know that but would ask questions just the same to put doubt in his mind that they were aware of anything.

***

In the UT there was movement and things would be brewing once again.

CHAPTER FIFTY-TWO

The Catlings were restless and could sense and smell something coming their way. They hid behind trees and watched and waited as several guards passed by with a large cart. They had seen this thing before and remembered how some of them were burned and permanently disfigured. They hesitated to move out in the open to investigate.

They waited until the last guard passed and attacked from the rear pulling two unsuspecting guards away.

The rest of the men gathered together and kept the cart in front of them for protection. The Head Guard pulled out one of the vials of the potion that Queen Beregina had given him. He hesitated at first to use it but had no other recourse. He cringed as he listened to the screams of the two men who had been pulled away by the Catlings. He had to do something.

As more Catlings came closer to the cart, he opened up the vial and splashed out some at the nearest Catling. He watched in horror as the Catling did not burn or move away. He couldn't believe his bewildered eyes.

The rest of the guards yelled out in alarm and ran for their lives as the Catlings chased them while the one that was touched by the potion stayed to attack the shocked Head Guard who had not moved because he was transfixed by this sight.

"How did that happen?" the Head Guard yelled out loud to no one. "I don't understand. The potion was not supposed to do that!"

The Catling edged closer as the Head Guard backed away, not taking his eyes off of the Catling that continued to lick the potion off his paws. The guard couldn't believe what he was seeing!

Spindle was sleeping in his treehouse when he heard the muffled screams at a distance. He also began to receive messages from his fellow Sprites who were closer to the sounds.

"Spindle, you need to come quickly. More of Parotovina's guards are in the UT. They are being hunted by the Catlings. You won't believe what we are seeing here."

"I'm on my way." Spindle said as he patted his sword and wondered if this was the time he would need to use it.

Spindle sent a message to the King to let him know that there was trouble in the UT and that he was going there to investigate.

Gateskin wasn't asleep but rather strategizing with his wife about his next move to help the dragon ladies and their parents if the need arose.

Solinara could sense that something was drastically wrong when she saw the look of concern on her husband's face.

"What did you hear, Gateskin?"

He quickly relayed the message from Spindle to his wife and rushed out the door to the UT.

"Stay safe, Gateskin. If you need me or anyone else's assistance, please tell me right away."

"I will, Solinara. Stay here with the children and keep them safe. I will message you soon."

Gateskin stood at the border and opened the barrier when he spotted Spindle flying above.

"What is it, Spindle?"

"You need to see this for yourself, King," Spindle stated, his voice shaking uncharacteristically.

Gateskin was not expecting this and blinked his eyes a few times to clear his vision at what he was seeing as the guards continued calling out for help.

NOT THE END YET

Stay tuned for the next book in this series!

ABOUT THE AUTHOR

Janice Spina is a retired administrative secretary from a public school system in Massachusetts. She has always loved writing poetry, novels and children's stories. She published her first book in 2013 and hasn't stopped since.

This is the 49th book Janice has published. She also has two mystery series of six books each, one for boys and the other for girls. They are enjoyed by both boys and girls. She has published 23 children's stories for young children. She also writes under J.E. Spina, and has published nine novels and a short story collection for 18+.

She can be reached at these links.

Website: https://Jemsbooks.com
Blog: https://Jemsbooks.blog
Twitter: https://twitter.com/janice_spina
FB Main Page:
https://facebook.com/janice.spina.9

FB Author Page:
https://facebook.com/janicespina7
FB Novelist Page:
https://facebook.com/jespina7

Janice lives in New Hampshire with her husband, John, and a tank of tropical fish. John is the illustrator of her children's books and designer of all her book covers.

If you enjoyed this book, please leave a review where you purchased it and spread the word to your family and friends. Janice loves to hear from readers and welcomes reviews from wherever her books are purchased. She says, 'It's like Christmas each time I receive a review!'

If you would like to be on Janice Spina's email list to receive updates, newsletters, and special deals on books, please follow her blog at link above.

Watch for more books coming from Jemsbooks.

A NOTE FROM THE AUTHOR

Book 1 of this series was written over ten years ago. At that time, I wasn't ready to publish it. There were too many other books I wanted to publish first. I've always enjoyed reading fantasy and wanted to create my own fantasy series for young adults. This is Book 4 in the continuing saga of *Gateskin Chronicles*.

This series is written for young adults – Ages 15+, but can be enjoyed by preteens and adults too. I consider this series to be PG-13 and up. It is up to parents to use their discretion about whether your children should read this series. Some things may not be suitable for younger children. There is never any vulgar language in any of my books but there are some situations that may be too violent for younger readers.

I hope you enjoyed this work of fiction. Watch for more books in this series coming over the next year or so.

Thank you for purchasing one of Jemsbooks. I appreciate your kind support of me and my books. If you like this book, a review would be greatly appreciated wherever you purchased it. Reviews and word of mouth are the best way to spread your thoughts about books. Please share your review with friends and family. I would love to hear from you. You can reach me at jjspina@comcast.net.

All my books are available on Amazon and Barnes & Noble. Watch for more books coming for all ages.

With Blessings & Love,

Janice Spina

YA BOOKS BY JANICE SPINA - PG 13+

The Legend of the Taken Ones (Gateskin Chronicles Book 1)

Mom's Choice Awards – Gold Medal

Book Excellence Award Finalist

The Unknown Territory (Gateskin Chronicles Book 2)

Mom's Choice Awards – Gold Medal

Maincrest Media Book Awards

Search for the Medallion (Gateskin Chronicles Book 3)

Mom's Choice Awards – Gold Medal

More books coming in the next year and beyond!

OTHER MG/PT/YA BOOKS BY JANICE SPINA - 10+

Davey & Derek Junior Detectives Book 1:

The Case of the Missing Cell Phone
Pinnacle Book Achievement Award,
Honorable Mention- Readers' Favorite
Book Award

Davey & Derek Junior Detectives Book 2:

The Case of the Mysterious Black Cat
Pinnacle Book Achievement Award

Davey & Derek Junior Detectives Book 3: The Case of the Magical Ivory Elephant

Pinnacle Book Achievement Award & Reader's
Favorite Book Awards – Silver Medal

Davey & Derek Junior Detectives Book 4: The Case of the Brown Scraggly Dog
Top Shelf Book Awards – First Place
Finalist in Red City Review Awards
5-Star Book Review – Readers' Favorite
Book Awards

Davey & Derek Junior Detectives Book 5:
The Case of the Sad Mischievous Ghost
Pinnacle Book Achievement Award
Authorsdb Cover Contest – Silver
Medal

Davey & Derek Junior Detectives Book 6: The Case of the Mystery of the Bells

Pinnacle Book Achievement Award, Finalist – Readers' Favorite Book Awards, Finalist – Book Excellence Awards

Abby & Holly School Dance
Pinnacle Book Achievement Award & Bronze Medal from Readers' Favorite Book Awards

Abby & Holly Series Book 2: Unfortunate Events
Pinnacle Book Achievement Award, Readers' Favorite Book Awards – Honorable Mention

Abby & Holly Series, Book 3, Secrets of the Trunk
Pinnacle Book Achievement Award

Abby & Holly Series, Book 4, The Hidden Stairway

Pinnacle Book Achievement Award

Abby & Holly Series, Book 5, The Copper Key

Pinnacle Book Achievement Award

Abby & Holly Series, Book 6, Faulty Timeline

Pinnacle Book Achievement Award

More MG/PT books coming over the next few years!

BOOKS BY J.E. SPINA FOR 15+

The Misunderstood Angel (Branyrd the Angel Series Book 1)

Five-Star review from Readers Favorite Book Award

Mission of Mercy (Branyrd the Angel Series Book 2)

Mission of Love (Branyrd the Angel Series Book 3)

Mission of Hope (Branyrd the Angel Series Book 4)

BOOKS BY J.E. SPINA FOR 18+

Hunting Mariah

Finalist in Authorsdb First Lines Contest

Main Crest Media Award

Mariah's Revenge

Finalist in Authorsdb First Lines Contest

How Far is Heaven

Five-Star review from Readers' Favorite Book Awards

An Angel Among Us: A Short Story Collection

In A Second

Lubelia Alycea: One Hundred Years

Five-Star review from Readers' Favorite
Book Awards